Toni Davidson is a writer, editor and performer. He has previously edited an anthology of Scottish lesbian and gay writing *And Thus Will I Freely Sing* (Polygon). His fiction has appeared in the *The Crazy Jig, The Mammoth Book of Gay Stories, Queer Words* and *Rebel Inc.* His performance work has been staged at the CCA and Arches Theatre in Glasgow.

Intoxication

An anthology of stimulant-based writing

··

EDITED BY TONI DAVIDSON

Library of Congress Catalog Card Number 97–062392

A complete catalogue record for this book can be obtained
from the British Library on request

First published in 1998 by Serpent's Tail
4 Blackstock Mews, London N4

Web site: http://www.serpentstail.com

Phototypeset in 10/12pt Times by Intype London Ltd
Printed in Great Britain by Mackays of Chatham

10 9 8 7 6 5 4 3 2 1

Contents

Acknowledgements

The editor would like to thank the following people who helped make this book a living breathing thing. Irvine Welsh, Kevin Williamson, Laurence O'Toole at Serpent's Tail, Cal King and Graham Bell of the Kingsborough Experience, and to Ian Hendry for the Love Experience.

'Where the Railway Meets the River' is extracted from the book *Gone Tomorrow* by Gary Indiana, © 1993 Gary Indiana, reprinted by permission of Hodder Headline and Pantheon Books, a division of Random House, Inc.

'Beats on the Beach' by Lynne Tillman was first published in the *Voice Literary Supplement*, 7 July, 1992.

Introduction

···

In my mind there is an image of Tennessee Williams. It is a black and white photograph taken by Karsh. The playwright is slumped over his typewriter, unshaven, dishevelled; his bleary eyes staring into some middle distance through a pall of cigarette smoke. When I first saw it, I took it as a celebration of the aesthetic of writing: Williams hunched over his 'tool' burdened by the elusive emergence of imagination. In short, I thought Williams looked every bit a writer. Of course, he was doped up to the eyeballs with a combination of uppers and downers.

There is a special relationship between writers and stimulants. De Quincey on opium, Baudelaire on hashish, Burroughs on speed, Huxley on mescaline – all writers fusing psychoactive drugs with the creative urge; blurring experimentation with need, desire with addiction. There is such a rich and varied history to stimulant-based writing that it would be easy to dwell on past glories – all of us destined to read *Fear and Loathing in Las Vegas* one last time, *The Doors of Perception* in our hands on our deathbeds – but there must also be a sense of moving on, of recognising that stimulant-based writing isn't a closed genre, lost in time, but rather a burgeoning influence on writers writing now. Without doubt there is a very real upsurge in such writing in the nineties. The canvas is so much broader now, in terms of both cultural influence – from clubs to music to film – and the increasing, almost mundane, unsensational aspect to recreational drug use.

Whether as imbiber or chronicler, cultural observer or reformed cynic, the writer is involved.

However, the last thing I would want to do is to present the writers in this anthology as a united front, a unified, collective imagination where stimulant-based writing means one and the same thing to all of them. Far from it. Just as Yves Navarre once said, 'I am gay, I am a writer, I am not a gay writer', similarly writers in this book may want to swerve away from some homogeneous identity, preferring as broad a perspective as they can achieve with their work. Tennessee Williams was just the start of it, the romantic vision of the writer enslaved, enraged by stimulants has splintered in the nineties hotpot of cultural evolution. And all for the better. Let's not tie ourselves in knots with fading caftans. Stimulant-based writing is no longer the preserve of unshaven men, speeding through the night, their fingers glued to the typewriter. We are discovering that women can be both acute observers of and active participants in drug culture, and allowing for this, accepting the increasingly multicultural aspects to stimulant-based writing, opens up a whole new perspective for the reader. In a similar vein, gay men have infused their own experiences into the hard-nosed, male debauchery syndrome so often witnessed and indulged in by writers.

This is not simply a celebratory collection, not everybody's hands are in the air, not everybody's mouths are shouting we don't care. The eclectic nature of the writing serves the notion that in diversity there is honesty. I wanted to go down as well as up and a little sideways. And ultimately there is a strong sense that stimulant-based writing, taking account of its past and its present myriad incarnations, is not simply a theme

....

grafted on to prose to appeal to a chemical generation but is a way of seeing, a way of recording and relating experiences, of exploring the unencumbered, uncensored imagination.

Toni Davidson
March 1997

Latitude 52

JEFF NOON

Having blown all hope of resurrecting my flagging career as a self-styled 'street-honed collector and purveyor in all things transformative', I concluded to make a fresh start in life. This latest decision to reinvent myself was funded by a certain incident involving four bottles of Pining Noir, five packs of Smoggies Extra Tar, and at least sixteen clamberings aboard the more than generous haunches of the frustrated wife of a local Member of Parliament, Sir William Scunthorpe Bingo IV.

Passion sure is stupid, when fuelled by chemicals. I was caught deliriously off-guard with my engine of generation in the council's first orifice (in election year, natch) and now I had Billy Bingo's pack of pinstriped slobbering minders snapping at my scent, hungry for retribution. Given this predicament, who wouldn't decide it was high time to cut their losses (before the losses included their own genitalia) and find some new position in the world?

So it was that I took the misbegotten advice of my sister, Gina, who had heard from a distant and famously unreliable source that a certain party were looking for someone 'bad to the bone' to complete their team of 'adventurers'. A tracker they were looking for, someone with the 'requisite lack of morals' needed in order to find a secret route out of New London. These reprobates wanted to go north, carrying some illicit cargo. My sister wouldn't say what the cargo was. 'One bad journey,' was all she grunted. 'It will make something of you, yes?' I was being offered a nothingness fuck in other words, a ride to nowhere, but what choice did I really have? Up to that point I had been nothing more than a most bitter and sour wastrel. Bad and boneless. 'You must be desperate to get me out of town, Gina,' I said. 'Is mother nearly dead, is that it?'

'How would you know anything at all about Mummy?'

'One of us had to leave, okay? Aren't you grateful?'

'All you do is steal her supplies.'

'Well that's all over now, isn't it? It's all yours, sis, you hear me? Take it and choke.'

'Just making sure, Eugene.'

'Uh-huh.'

'The travellers want you now. Or else you'll be castrated, yes? I could give your secret address to Sir Billy Bingo MP?'

A moment's breath.

'Okay, sis. Give me the digits.'

There was once a crazy girl, Alice her name, who loved to dream her days away and to climb inside mirrors. She had the strangest adventures in mirrorland, and very soon she became hopelessly obsessed with being turned topsy-turvy. Real life was so very dull and boring that Alice could no longer resist becoming her own perverted reflection; again and again she climbed into the mirror. Her schoolwork began to suffer, as did her physical well-being. Her once golden skin turned ashen, her eyes bled a map of sorry veins. Every time she reversed herself out of the looking glass, she promised never to go there again. But how could she possibly give up such wonderings? Then, one time, her father caught her in the act of reversing herself. He slapped

....

her and called her a terrible name, and in his anger he sent his prized antique paperweight sailing through the air. Explosion! The mirror shattered into twelve jagged pieces. All the glittering shards of a dream, falling over the lost and weeping Alice . . .

That's the story my father told me, just before his chosen death. 'We're all addicts, aren't we,' he said, 'in one way or another? Whether to substances legal or illegal, dope or coke or gin or coffee, love or lust, living dirty, living clean, or even to mirrors and what we see behind the smile. We all have our fix of choice, the dream that sets us off and keeps us going. The drug that kills us. We're all addicted to something stranger than ourselves. Choose wisely, my child.'

I guess I wasn't listening too good.

There was a demo going on outside the Pig and Tapeworm, a purely members-only establishment famous for its 'no muckiness' policy. The protesters were a bunch of torn-jeaned Mucky Fronters, calling for an end to alcoholic apartheid. Faced against these chaos-merchants were the supporters of Billy Bingo's Purity Party. 'A vote for William Bingo, a vote for freedom.' Yeah sure, the freedom to wear a suit in the streets, and nothing else but. Freedom to Belong. And I had to run this gauntlet just to have a quiet fucking drink with some potential business partners!

I was wearing my powder-pink demob suit. Of course, I hadn't actually taken part in the last Share Wars, but a man can dream, can't he? No way mucky, but a long haul from a shiny-arsed blue-and-white business affair. I had a spot of bother with the doorman, but he acquiesced when I mentioned my appointment. Maybe these adventurers actually carried some weight.

'Are you the tracker, by any chance?' a zebra-kitted

. . . .

guy asked from the foggy depths of the pub. He was pushing fifty, like pushing against a wall. A faceful of creases, the map of deep life.

'Maybe,' I answered. I was led along to a table, where another person, a woman, was waiting. They were drinking Burpington's Weightless and smoking Menthol Sloths. Drugless drugs. Not my kind of people.

'Eugene Maguire, am I right to assume?' the guy insisted.

'I told you already.'

'Please be seated. Would you perchance desire a pint of beer?'

'I don't drink beer. Get me a Pining Noir.' Pining Noir was French for Black Regret, a deep and red gene-wine that stirred some vicious changes in the old DNA. My mother's invention. So don't ask me why I'm addicted, okay?

The guy sauntered over to the bar, leaving me with the woman. Total silence. She was about my age, twenty-one or so. Looking ill, in ill-fitting pinstripe, like a suit of disguise. Bad vibes and not a word of greeting. I offered her Smogline ciggies, triple tar; politely refused. 'Please yourself.' I lit up, took a deep, life-changing drag. Some straightlacers at a nearby table wrinkled a nose or two. 'What's the score, then?' The woman turned her gaze over to some fascinating shape on the flock wallpaper. 'We shall await Lurcher's return.' End of story. Let us wait.

Lurcher returned with my drink. 'They don't serve wine in here,' he told me. 'Too mucky. So I got you a boring beer. Now then, let me make the intros. Bob Lurcher's the name. And this is Lonely Mondo . . .'

The woman smiled, a tiny curving of her lips.

Oh, she was lonely, was she? Now there's an opening. A striking beauty, for all that loneliness, sweet-boned

. . . .

and with a sunburst finish of curling red and blonde hair. Too much to look at. Way too much.

'We want you for your tracking knowledge,' Lurcher whispered over his beer. 'You can do it?'

'Do what?' I asked.

'Find us a path to the North.'

'The North is difficult.'

'You've been there?'

'Sure, I've been north.'

'How far?'

'Watford Gap.'

'You ever go above Latitude 52? Through the Wall?'

'Milton Keynes? Don't be silly.'

'Never been to Manchester?'

'Manchester? That's one big fuck-hole. Good-bye.'

The Mondo woman was smiling at me the whole time. I had to turn back somewhat, to gaze at that welcome smile. The crimson-beauty of her lips. 'You think Manchester is dangerous?' Lurcher asked, forcing me back down.

'Manchester is more than dangerous,' I answered; 'there's no laws up there.'

'Sure thing, Eugene; in chaos lies fortune. You don't like the sniff of dosh?'

'Okay. What's so special? What's the delivery?'

'Top secret, what?'

'Drugs, huh? Something tasty? So you're Muckies, right?'

'Just get us through the wall, old bean. We do the rest.'

'But, Manchester?' I cried. 'Nobody's been there for years.'

'But I would've thought . . . with your connections . . .'

'I don't have connections. Not any more.'

'Not Eugene Maguire, heir apparent to the Mag Flux

. . . .

millions? Makers of the Black Regret and the Smog-line? The makers of Latitude fucking 52! and the first-born doesn't have any connections? Why, you've been thieving supplies from the family's warehouse for the last seven years, and sending them northwards. Oh yes, I've been doing my research. Your father was actually *born* in Manchester. No connections, Eugene? Really?'

'It's all dried up. The family found my supplier.'

'So you don't want the job?' said Lonely.

I turned to her, as best I could. 'Sure,' I replied, 'I really want to commit suicide.'

'Lonely and I are the new breed,' announced the Lurcher. 'We're the Hyper-Muckies.'

'Was that hyper or diaper?'

'We look good, we talk good, we can get away with infiltration, and it gives me great pleasure to parade myself within this port of purity. But deep down inside we're just the latest deliverers of dirt. I hear street rumours you're the same, tracker man. Are you denying your true nature?'

I gave Lurcher my best back-off-buddy shrug, but really he was hitting my worst spot. I guess the two-faced life was grinding me down.

'Fair enough if Bingo gets to be Prime Minister,' Lurcher continued. 'Fair enough and serves you right. When he gets in, you'll be on the good-bye list, along with all of us. You really want to visit that cemetery?'

'No way will it happen,' I tried. 'Bingo is doomed. The people won't vote for tight genes.' From the outside, we could hear the demo getting nasty.

'The people, the people!' Lurcher cried. 'The people are ready to be ruled by a pinstripe! The people are fed up with muckiness; they want to be controlled, controlled completely. That is their snivelling want!' Lurcher brought his head real close to mine, going some total Mucky distance, the good language falling

....

away. 'The truth is,' he breathed, 'all of us around this table are way beyond that controlling shit. I'm including you, Eugene. I'm thinking you're unhappy with your current guise. I'm thinking you want to declare yourself. The sniff of escape. Doesn't that dirty aroma smell lovely? I'll bet your old man had a whiff of that, just before – ?'

'Okay, shut up! What do I get out of it?'

'You've been tupping Bingo's good lady wife, I hear? Now that is naughty. That's to be celebrated. Let's cut some rug.' He stood up, glided over to the centre of the room. I watched in disbelief as he started to chant: 'Long live muckiness! Death to the pinstripe!'

'Digging it!' snarled Lonely Mondo in tune. 'Long live the Mucky Front!'

They'd both gone total arse-to-the-wind. The pure-hearted punters were covering up their ears and screaming at the dirty words. 'Lurcher!' I cried, 'The cops – !'

'Let them come!'

Everything went megacrazy then; a whirl of chaos that played a twister. The Mucky Fronters were trying to storm the place, led on by the pirate calls from within. A call to arms. They burst into the club, trampling the bouncers. Fighting broke out, until the sirens of the Pure Cops came wailing down the streets. The punters, the pinstripers, the Bingo-players and the Fronters, they all ran for the exits. Lurcher and his lovely cohort simply vanished. I wish I knew that trick.

My prints and body fluids were matched to a complaint filed by Sir William Scunthorpe Bingo IV, leader of the nation's Purity Party, and the bookies' fave for the upcoming role of PM. And when that cuckolded man was thick with promises of increasing the Cop funds by twenty-five per cent . . .

....

Well, the words 'deep' and 'shit' start to get mightily conjoined.

I spent a bad night in the cells, pushing off the wandering libidos of my fellow prisoners. I got no sleep, but plenty of time to think. *The wall, the wall, the bleeding wall at Latitude 52.* My father's most celebrated, most hated invention. It split good old England exactly in two, along the great divide. Good old Tom Maguire had built it to keep out the ravenous Northern Hordes; it also stopped anyone escaping from the South. Nobody knew how it worked, exactly, especially since my father had killed himself by driving headlong into it. What was I supposed to do? Escape through the Latitude . . .

Jesus in pieces! That wall was deadly.

Some unknown benefactor came to my rescue the next morning. The cops were paid off with some choice bottles of gene-wine, billions of Smoggies and a whole fistful of weighted money. I watched the cops fooling around with the wine and the ciggies and the Eurodosh as I walked through the station's doors.

Freedom. Blessed air . . .

Two hours later (dazed and sizzling with bus-rage) I arrived back in my dingy flat in Notting Hill, with the hope of a long and cooling bath. The minders of Billy IV had beaten me to it. The flat was one uncool mess. A Bingobomb aftermath. Magneted to the fridge was a message, written in quasi-dogshit. 'We be hungry. Signed, upon this day, Woof and the Tweeter.'

Woof and the Tweeter?

Let me off the world, please! Of course, but known only to the wise, the real reason Billy Bingo was after pinstriping me was that I had cut in on his business. Nothing to do with his loving wife. That's right. Bingo was a drug-dealer, *par excellence.* This will not be

. . . .

featured in his manifesto. I was his rival in the game
of selling transformative dreams. But while he was a
covert dealer hiding behind politics, I was an open
shop, hidden only by my conscience. No wonder he
hated me.

And somebody had shopped me to him. That was
the only truth I could gather from my flat-mess. Shit to
fuck! Minder-hounds had invaded my space. I'd been
found out. Super-suckered. And I knew exactly who to
blame.

My money was panting a dying breath from my
wallet, thanks to the cops; they'd confiscated what little
resources I had, leaving me with just half a crown to
my credit. One third of which I'd already blown on
bus-fare. I spent a few desolate minutes trying to cool
my flat back to its former state of being. This is when
I discovered that the minders of Bingo had stolen my
last remaining stash of goodies. My nest egg for a rainy
day, and was it forever raining. I had nothing to sell,
nothing to trade, nothing left to live for. No overproof
gene-wine, no bootleg ciggy-dreams, no crazy way
forward.

A sudden noise startled me.

Shit! What was that? Phone! Calm down, cool out.
Gave me a little shock, that's all. The thing grabbed:
'Who's that?' Said quickly.

'It's myself, darling brother.'

'You shopped me to Bingo, Gina.'

'Well I was having to, yes? Otherwise you'd not be
moving anywhere.'

'Cow fuck!'

'Why so ungrateful, Eugene? I don't want you killed
or arrested, or anything else so bad.'

'No, you just want me out of the picture.'

'Mother is wanting a little word.'

'What?' Now that really threw me wide open; I

....

9

hadn't spoken to mother since my running away. What did she want now? This tiny breathing over the wires, a mumble of words, old and parched and rasping from a deathbed:

'Eugene, my favourite . . .'

I wanted to tell her that I wasn't her favourite anymore, but the words wouldn't come clean, faced with that fever.

'Eugene, I hear you're planning to leave.'

I wanted to tell her I was being *forced* to leave, but the words were stuttered.

'I forgive you, my child.'

I wanted to ask what the forgiveness was for.

'For stealing my products, and reselling them at a profit. I forgive you. Pay no attention to Gina. Didn't I get you free from the police?'

'That was you?' At last, I could speak. 'You did that?'

'A little bribery, that's all. Don't waste my love, Eugene. Please don't. I'm not long for this world, my son. Please be careful. Don't let the wall take you. Don't be like your father.'

Of course I won't – Shit! What was that? A noise from outside.

'Hang on, mother.' My last ever words to her, heralded by a clanging noise from the street below. I peeped through a gap in the curtains. Down in the street a pair of Bingo's minders were slouched against the bonnet of a dogmobile. The slobberhounds, Woof and the Tweeter, no doubt. One of them even waved at me, like teasing a cat, you know? The other was mangling a street sign with a sledgehammer. That was the noise. Maybe it was a time to be young again.

So I bade a hasty farewell to the old flat forever. Slipped out of the back window, landing on a kitchen's extension roof, from there to the yard floor and the

. . . .

back gate. Let the minders come visit; they would find only empty air, and sad and lost and lonely dreams. With the telephone still singing, my mother's voice, drifting into distant signals, 'Eugene? Are you there, my child? What's happening?' Don't even think about it.

Another runaway. How many can there be in one lonely life?

Five hours later I was rattling along in the back of a brand new Earth Rover van. Four-wheel jive and the gravity brakes; vampire lamps and a turbo-mother and the whole kit, the kitchen sink. All the EcoVaz petrol the tank could hold. Long-range potential and guns on the bumper. A most excellent getaway vehicle. Painted on its sides, the logo of the Wall Menders, a glistening portcullis. Lonely Mondo was in the back with me; Lurcher up front, driving.

Silence all over the Rover, except for the cries from outside, the screams and night-shouts of the Seven Sisters Road. London North. And the further north we went, the more ragged was the populace, the darker the night, like the genetic purity was weaker at the edges.

Sure thing, we were heading upwards and out of the rulings.

Escaping . . .

The Lonely woman was giving me occasional words, for sure, but nothing more than splinters. I was trying to work out the relationship between this ignoble pair. Were Lurcher and Lonely lovers? Or else they hated each other, and this was purely business? Or else they were father and daughter; now there was a thought. Certainly, there was little passion to be wasted between them, and this feeling raged against my soul.

'Are you weakening, Eugene?'

. . . .

11

'What?'

'You look worried.' Lonely's voice, at last, asking me some real questions.

'No. I'm fine,' I answered, making an effort. 'Why do you ask?'

'Just wondering.'

'Wonder no more.'

'Why did you run away?'

'What?' It was all I could say.

'You ran away from home,' she said. 'Away from the Mag Flux. Away from such a family fortune. I was just wondering why, that's all.'

'Leave me alone.' A cry from nowhere. Then she looked at me, full on with those singing eyes. What else could I do but give in. 'I left because of my father. You've done the research, Lonely. Yeah, I killed him.'

'That's not quite true.'

'Okay. Assisted suicide, the jury called it. What difference does it make?'

'It's what he wanted. Wine and cigarettes.'

'Yeah. A real overdose on his own product. Way to go.'

'Is that how you'll die, Eugene?'

'Shit, I was only fourteen years old. What's a kid supposed to do when his father asks for escape. Yeah, I helped him with the dosage, when he was too weak to take it himself. I fed those cigs into his lungs, I swilled that wine down his throat. Then I helped him into his car, started the engine, set him going. I even waved him good-bye. Do you think I'm proud?'

'You got away with it.'

'I got two years suspended. He was already dead, I guess, before he hit the wall at the 52nd parallel.'

'Now you're heading the same way.'

'We all are.'

'Why did he do it?'

....

'Why does anybody? He was sick of the business. Sick of love. He wanted out. And the wall was calling to him, that's what he mumbled. We're all addicts, in one way or another. – Isn't that fair?'

'No, I mean why did he build the wall? I mean, he was born in Manchester, wasn't he? What was he scared of?'

'I don't know.'

'So you killed him, and then you ran away?'

'What else could I do?'

'They say that Latitude 52 takes your soul for a building block.'

'They say a thousand things.'

'Let's hit that wall, Eugene. Find us the sweetest thrill.'

I almost kissed her then. Almost. So very, very almost. I guess I could've loved that lonely woman of the sunburst, given another life, another planet, another universe. Another, cleaner mother and father.

Another dream.

At a certain point, halfway to the London limits, Lurcher called me, urging me to come join him up front. Lonely had dropped off to sleep. I had to carefully extricate myself from her lolling shape as I made the journey. Lurcher said nothing at first. His eyes were glued to the road ahead. Driving through darkness. There were no streetlamps out here, no biocat's eyes to lead the way. We were riding through the barren lands that surrounded Greater New London. The moon was a sliver of lemon tarting up the black sky. Through the van's window I watched acres of nothingness roll by. Landscape of my empty soul and stomach, my various journeys to nowhere. My roguish life up till then. And after ten minutes of this monotonous interface, I finally

....

spoke up: 'What's with the Wall Mender's Earth Rover, Lurch?'

'Fence Defencing,' Lurcher replied; 'that's our logo-disguise, old chap. According to our passports we're just a bunch of imagineers. The good wall needs a little maintenance, now and again, don't you know? It's all been worked out.'

'You're going to get that past the guards?'

'Watch me.'

Through the Watford Gap . . .

I was just about to ask Lurcher for my initial payment when we came to a roadblock in the middle of nowhere. Lights were playing games over our vehicle, and a pair of cops were manning the station. An illuminated sign read CHECKPOINT CHARLES III. Lurcher pulled up at the No-Go sign. The big wall waited somewhere beyond, painting the world with limit.

A she-cop stuck her head through the side-window. 'What's your business this far north?' She had the full gear; the fire-gun, the X-ray specs, the sponsor logos on her uniform. Pure Burger Cops. Keeping New London free of additives. 'Breaches in the wall, officer,' Lurcher answered, showing his papers.

The she-cop made one more pass over the vehicle and its sorry occupants, and then said, finally, 'Pass along, my friends. Make the Purity good.'

'You bet your life, officer.' Lurcher's words, as he drove through the checkpoint. And as soon as we were free, 'Fucking good stuff! They fell for it.' Lonely had slept through all this, like nothing bad ever happened. Maybe, just maybe, mind, this pair of outlaws could pull me clean.

Five minutes and a lifetime of driving, during which Lurcher's eyes were steely-fixed upon the empty world unfurling in his beams. We were watching the night flit by in rags of pitch and an occasional blasted tree. An

. . . .

abandoned car passing in an instant of burnt colours, while up ahead the wall was starting to shimmer with flames, stretching the horizon, end to end like a frequency. A quick look over my shoulder; Lonely was still asleep. 'So what is it with you two?' I whispered to the driver. 'I mean, I'm curious, that's all.'

'We had a thing going on,' Lurcher slowly answered, 'Ages ago, mind. But since we got the hyper-mode working, I don't know . . .'

'So you ditched her?'

'I'm her manager.'

'What's she selling?'

'Love. What else?'

'You're her pimp? Jesus!'

'Such a coarse word, Eugene. We're all selling something. Lonely has a grand talent. You can partake, if you so desire. As long has you pay for it.'

'No thanks.'

'Maybe in Manchester, we can both find our chosen creatures?'

I don't know, maybe I'm the last human to ask about love. I couldn't stop thinking about my father's last message: *We're all addicts, in one way or another. Choose wisely, my child.* The Wall had been his last choice, but there have been so many addictions in my own life . . . how could I possibly choose between them all? 'What are we delivering, Lurch?' I asked the driver.

'Open the glove compartment,' he answered.

'There's nothing in there.'

'Press the catch. At the back.'

'Here?'

'That's it. Slide the panel out. That's it.'

So I pulled a nondescript wooden box from the glove compartment.

. . . .

'That's my beauty,' Lurcher said. 'Look inside. Be careful, now.'

I opened up the lid. Inside was a bundle of velvet cloth, wrapped around something hard. I started to unwrap the cloth, using my left hand. Yeah, I was born a southpaw and sinister. 'Be careful!' Lurcher's voice, harsh as he drove. 'Don't look too deeply.' Inside the cloth was a shard of glass. No, not glass; silvered glass, the fragment of a mirror. Jagged and extreme, it caught a light from nowhere, reflected it back a thousand-fold. I was almost blinded. 'I told you not to look too deeply!' Lurcher almost drove us into a ditch as he shouted at me. 'Fuck!'

'What is it?'

'How would I know?' As he righted the van by sheer willpower. 'We have to deliver it to Manchester, to a woman called Emma Pleasance. She's a collector; big money for the dispatch. That's all I know. And not to look into it. Okay?'

You don't say. So I wrapped the piece of mirror back into its covering, back into the box, back into the space behind the dashboard. The van went dark again. 'Now do you understand,' asked Lurcher, 'why I'm so fired up?'

'I guess so.'

Of course, I knew exactly what it was, that sliver of reflecting glass. There was once a crazy girl, Alice her name, who loved to dream her days away and to climb inside mirrors. Until, one time, her father caught her in the act of reversing herself. He slapped her hard, called her a terrible name, and then sent his silver paperweight sailing through the air. Explosion! The mirror shattered into twelve jagged pieces. Rare prizes. All the broken shards of a dream, falling over the lost and weeping Alice. Collectors, over the years, have

....

searched long and hard to find those fragments of another world, paying superdosh for the sparkle doorways. Good money for a looking glass.

I have held such a glittering prize, and we're all addicts, aren't we, in one way or another? We're all addicted to something stranger than ourselves.

Please choose wisely.

So I gave some vague directions to Lurcher. He headed the van towards a little place in the wall I was certain was open. Fairly certain, anyway. I'd done my homework, worked my contacts. There were openings in the wall, of course. Well, not quite openings, more like weak spots. Where a drugs delivery could sneak through.

I was on a promise, a fully paid-for promise, out of future profits. Lupus Malone was due to meet us, the appointed time and place. Lupus was a wall-walker, one of those lonely souls that worked the boundaries between the here and gone. Lupus knew all the weak spots, all the openings. He was just an element of that long and complex food chain that connected the supplier to the addict, the addict way up north.

But I was scared, you know? I mean, my real job was just to steal the basic goods from the family firm, the wine and the ciggies, soup them up to illegal limits. Wait for the payback. It wasn't my job to actually make the goddamn delivery! That was for the reckless. But here I was, on the edge of civilisation, hoping for a clean breakthrough. Heading for the place my father had crashed himself into nothingness. 'Okay, stop the van, Lurch. This is where we wait.'

The legendary Latitude 52, located at the artificial town of Milton Keynes: Robotown. Where the South ended. Lurcher killed the engine, and the night breathed a fume of desire. Not a soul disturbed the

....

ghostly streets. The moon went whispering behind a sodden cloud.

Not a feather stirred the air.

'Okay, tracker-boy, earn your passage.' Lurcher's orders.

Lonely Mondo woke up as the van stopped. She popped her head forward, to witness the wall. 'Ahhh!' It was certainly quite magnificent, that wall of numbers, in all its limiting power. I swear I could see myself, looking back at myself, from the wall's shiny surface. Like a global mirror. But it wasn't real, the wall, I knew that much from my contacts and the rumours. The wall was a dream-thing, a separation point, where one world bled off into the next. A mere illusion, coloured with glimmers of starlight and snatches of cries. The wall was weeping. Salty tears that could kill. The boundary always took a sacrifice, for the right of passage. A single random victim, from all those passing through. Life's a gamble, right? The more travelling companions you have, the greater your chance of escape. My father had driven alone through the interface. That's a sucker's bet.

'Where's your fucking walker?' Lurcher asked. 'You promised me – '

'He'll be here. Stay cool.'

'Fuck your cool. We want some delivery.'

As all around the van, shadows crept and lingered, on streets long forgotten. Ten minutes we waited, in a darkening silence. Way past the delivery date. Lurcher was starting to curse, Lonely was urging us to just drive forwards anyway. I guess she hated stillness. 'If it's true,' she said, 'that the wall keeps the crashees alive, maybe your daddy's waiting for you there – '

'Fuck off, Lonely!'

Who said that? Who just swore right then? That was me, swearing at Lonely Mondo for being so stupid.

....

'There's no such rumour,' I ventured. 'Now get back to sleep.' And so we waited some more, in a dreadful silence. Until –

'No travellers wanted!' Booming loud, sudden, a loaded voice. Transmitted from an antique robo that came trundling up to our vehicle, out of a long-range shadow, gun-hand creaking to target.

'Robo-shit!' cried Lurcher. Some other old and run-down robots were gathering around the Rover, a tribe of rusty guardians, left over from the whine of life. Lurcher trained the van's rotating guns upon them.

'Okay,' I breathed. 'Don't panic. Don't scare them. Act normal.'

'I *am* acting normal!' This from Lurcher.

'What's happening, Eugene?' This from Lonely Mondo. 'Are we in trouble?'

'Just act normal.'

'I'm trying to.'

Milton Keynes had once been the new vision of New England, back when new visions were newly real. Now all lay abandoned, and the town was a final outpost of reality, its gridwork of streets peopled only by dust and smoke and out-of-date, barely alive machines. Maybe these *apparati* surrounding us, maybe they had a half-ounce of humanity to share between them. At the very most. I could see nipples gasping for an oil-fix. They hadn't had a good feed in years, running on a program and a prayer. These were the starving bouncers. The night-watchmen of the soul. Neglected by society. But all of them had guns, and all of them were questioning our presence at the limits.

That's when we saw Lupus Malone. The wall-walker was being brought towards us, offered up like a sacrifice, spiked on a pair of sharpened robotic arms. His body was still twitching, gibbering, still dying. 'We're legal!' shouted Lurcher to the machines, waving his

....

official papers around. 'We've come to mend the fence. Believe me!' The first roboguard bumped against our side. Up close, I could see the rust forming on its mechanisms, and the dribbles of saliva on its parched lips. In a screechy voice, it was demanding a passport. Lurcher felt his well-planned disguise being clutched away from him. 'Man shit!' he growled, totally mucky. Several other robots had now trained their ancient pistols on the van. 'Papers don't compute,' they were squeaking. 'Please explain yourselves.'

Lurcher fired the van's bumper-guns, blowing at least two of the robots away, a storm of components. Only to see more and more of the creatures replace the fallen ones. 'Negative recognition,' one of the new guards croaked in a metallic voice, a bone-dry cocking. 'Security breach!'

'Eugene, do something!' shouted Lurcher.

'Like what?'

'Negative allowance!' tittered another robot as Billy Bingo came out of the shadows, Woof and the Tweeter behind him, walking away from a parked dogmobile. All three of them were smiling, like tomorrow was dead already. 'Prepare to be pinstriped.' Bingo's smile vanished as he gave the order and all the guns turned on us.

'It's a fucking set-up!' I shouted. 'Drive, Lurcher! Towards the wall!'

'Won't that kill us?'

'One of us. Only one. Or else we get – '

Or else we get burned. A cigarette lighter floating, so slowly, through the air. Robo-oil, catching fire. Lurcher sent that blazing van straight towards the wall, all alive with misty light. Middle England; Latitude 52. Through the fucking glass. While some lonely bullets penetrated the back window, slowly, quite slowly, made tepid by the wall's thick glue and the tendrils of a

....

dream. As we passed through the interface. It felt like being smothered, being overwhelmed, becoming someone else. Cries came to us. The bullets fell into the van like jellies. Lonely Mondo was able to catch one of them in her lazily outstretched hand. There was a deep pain in my stomach as the van slowed down and then kicked forward. Somebody somewhere ... somebody was screaming. I think it was me. It sounded like my father. Or was it my father's crash, long ago remembered?

Hours went by, in a mist. I was sitting on a wrought-iron bench, in a desolate park, on the very edge of Manchester. The van was parked nearby, portcullis logo scorched by burn marks. Somehow I had driven it this far, God only knows how. A dark blind drive it must have been, for I could remember little of the passage. I was hungry and parched, cold and lonely to the core and tired. Dawn came up so slowly, I was almost lost in the process. I had the wooden box on my lap. My last ever possession, except for a couple of hardline Smoggies, one of which I smoked down to the finger-tips. Then I opened the box, unwrapped the velvet cloth, using my right hand this time, northpaw and dextrous.

I looked deep into the fragment of mirror. I saw a lobster playing a banjo; I saw a magnet making love to itself; I saw a house of swords, a horse of Morse, a maw of paws. I saw a crazy little girl playing chess with a compass. I saw myself reflected, over and over, with a glimpse of my sunken eyes, heavy red with broken veins from taking one too many escaping drugs. It was a struggle to pull myself back out, before going too far.

Just let me make this one last ever delivery.

The wall was supposed to take only one for its payment, that was my father's ruling. What had gone

....

wrong? Why had it taken both Lonely and Lurcher? Why had it left me alone?

Weighted with reflections, I walked back to the van, drove it slow into Manchester Central, searching the living map. The Free Trade Hall passed me by, Old Trafford Football Ground passed me, the Hacienda nightclub passed me. Famous landmarks, read about in histories. All I had to do was find this Emma Pleasance woman, this no doubt doshed-up collector, deliver the dream, and then find myself a new life on the glorious proceeds. Become a Pure Citizen, or something; no more addictions, no more easy ways out. The van gave up the ghost of petrol, stuttered to a full stop. There was a major post office alongside, just about opened for the new day's messages. Marriot's Court, Manchester. Looking in a local directory there, I found sixteen addresses with the name Pleasance, Emma, Miss. One of them was the Pig and Tapeworm pub. I was confused by that, but maybe they had a franchise in Manchester. Maybe, but I doubt it; it was the exact same address, Central London!

There was once a crazy boy, Eugene his name, who loved to dream his days away and to climb inside mirrors.

Reeling backwards, I staggered out of the post office. The van was gone, and I thought it stolen at first, until I remembered the empty tank. Topsy-turvy, the Houses of Parliament towered over me, likewise the Cathedral of St Paul and the Palace at Buckingham. Some mad nutter was screeching a manifesto from Hyde Park corner; he looked very much like Billy Bingo MP, down on his luck. A couple of slobberers passed a hat around the thinning crowd. Pearly Kings sang about going up the old apples and pears, while a

....

bright red double-decker bus trundled by, KNOTTING HELL for its destination.

Ah, when I think of the juice that once fuelled me.

There is no Manchester. Latitude 52 is just a looking glass, and I was the chosen one. So I took a black cab to the Pig and Tapeworm, paying the driver with my last New London shilling. The King's head was reversed on the coin, coldly smiling to the right-hand side. The cab dropped me outside the pub, no demo this time. The Mucky Front bouncers let me through easily, totally accepting my powder-pink demob number: 'Right this way, Mr Maguire, sir; your party awaits you.' The pub was running wild, a thousand punters drinking my mother's best vintage and smoking their hearts out. My father appeared out of the fog.

'Miss Emma Pleasance?' I said.

'What took you so long?' he asked, taking the wooden box from my hands, and leading me to a vacant table, where a full bottle and a pack of twenty awaited.

....

Space Junk

JOHN KING

Rambo didn't like drinking with junkies. In fact, he hated them like nothing else on the planet. He considered drug addicts the lowest form of vermin, self-obsessed and dependent on artificial stimulants. He sipped his pint. They had no standards. The lager was flat but he drank it anyway. He needed the alcohol because the loser coming across the pub with a glass of lemonade, ice and lemon, was heading his way. The drugged-up cunt. The junky sat down and smiled that stupid smile he saved for old mates. Not that they were great friends, just Rambo's old girl had been on at him to take the sad little tosser out for a beer.

—How's life treating you then, Greg?

Greg sat down and sipped his lemonade. Rambo watched the bubbles rise inside the glass. A girl's drink. Cunt. He shouldn't be seen out and about with scum like this. It didn't look good.

—Not bad, Rambo. Not bad at all.

Was that it then? Was that fucking it? Greg was going to be hard going. There was a bit of a silence as Rambo lifted the glass to his mouth. Fucking shit lager. He looked around the pub. A kitted-out bird sat at the bar, staring into the mirror opposite with the Sky logo. She looked a bit of all right and had a nice body. He fancied a shag, but was lumbered with Greg, that fucking junky cunt from down the street.

—Must be four or five years since I last saw you,

Greg. What've you been doing with yourself. Not married yet? Shacked up with a woman?

Greg's face reddened.

—Haven't done much of anything. Still working at Radford's. Still dossing in the same flat. It's six years since I saw you, just before you went up to Scotland to work on the rigs. It was down the Pipemaker's. Remember? We were pissed and you were telling me to chat up that girl with the peroxide hair.

Rambo thought back. Greg was right. She'd been game enough, but the useless bastard didn't have the bottle. Rambo ended the evening getting a knee-trembler off her round the back of Tesco's. He'd forgotten about that. Six years. A long time.

—*Something* must've happened. Six years doesn't pass without some event catching the attention. Haven't you been off on holiday, poked a few birds along the way?

—It's hard to think really.

They used to call him Square Eyes. He was always watching the telly. TV junky. Must've watched six or seven hours each evening. Cunt just sat there staring into the machine while Rambo went off and made himself a packet. He'd worked hard and spent his money enjoying life, while Greg rotted away in front of the idiot box. TV was another fucking drug. It knocked the bloke out and kept him sedated.

—Remember we used to call you Square Eyes?

Greg blushed again. It was like he was in love with the fucking thing. A right fucking space cadet. It was in his blood now. No escape.

—You still sit in front of the telly in the evenings, Greg? Plugged into the medicine chest letting the current run through your veins, radiation seeping into your brain, killing the cells and turning them to mush.

....

—Yeah. I'm still there. Bolt upright with my finger in the socket.

The cheeky cunt puffed his chest out like a charged-up pigeon. Square Eyes was proud of his addiction. Rambo felt outraged as he emptied his glass. The bastard would be ages with the lemonade, so he went to the bar and bought himself another drink, changing brands. He stood next to the tasty bird at the counter and caught her eye in the mirror. He'd fuck the arse off that, no problem.

—You're Rambo, aren't you?

Rambo tried to put a name to the face. No chance. He tried putting a face to the body. Impossible.

—You don't remember me, do you?

—Course I do.

—No you don't. Don't worry, I won't hold it against you.

Rambo was straining the old grey matter trying to work out who the fuck she was, though he was certain he'd never seen her before. She must know a mutual friend. It was a lucky break, though, because she was a good-looker and well horny by the way she was giving him the eye, looking him up and down like he was going cheap in a sale. If he got in here he'd give that dodgy cunt Greg the brush-off. Square-eyed wanker.

—Six years ago, it was. I was drinking in the Pipe-maker's and you gave me a fine line of chat and we went down behind Tesco's. I had marks on my bum for a week after. You don't remember, do you?

—Of course I remember. Your hair's different now, that's all. Sorry about your arse. It was a difficult angle, propping you up on the dustbins like that.

—You kept calling me a dirty junky. Remember?

—Don't recall that, but I was well pissed. I went up to Scotland soon after. Went to work on the rigs.

Rambo was thinking back. That was right. She'd had

....

wicked-looking bruises on her arms. He could see them glowing in the dark. He'd forgotten all about that, he was so pissed. Bit dangerous, though, with AIDS and everything. Still, she looked healthy enough now, and it was six years ago. She was still breathing.

—It was a good laugh, wasn't it? At first you were telling that funny little mate of yours to come over and chat me up, but he was too shy I suppose. You were really mouthy and the whole pub could hear you telling him that I looked like a good fuck, your voice echoing through the speakers.

—Do you want a drink?

Rambo paid the extra for half a sweet cider.

—It's a coincidence that I've bumped into you now, because I'm seeing the same bloke tonight. Over there. The one with his eyes fixed on the telly. He's got a bad habit. No offence like. Sorry about that. Nothing wrong with a bit of drug addiction.

—I've been clean for years.

Rambo wanted to clap his hands. He was in. Safe and sound. Greg didn't turn round to see what was taking him so long. He was concentrating on Coronation Street, or EastEnders. The images were relayed through a massive set propped up on a specially designed shelf. Rambo pulled a stool up next to the woman. He wondered how she remembered his name after all this time. It was odd they met now and that she'd recognised him.

—What about your mate?

—Don't worry about him, he's long gone. Just waiting for the cremation. He's got every programme screened in the last twenty-eight years whizzing through his brain. He doesn't know what's real and what's not. He went down the superhighway years before they even thought of the Internet. Shot into the

....

twilight zone at warp factor 15 and he's been in orbit ever since.

—You can't just leave him like that.

—He doesn't mind. Anyway, he's not a mate. A friend of the family. The old girl kept on at me to take him for a drink because he doesn't get out much. She feels sorry for him.

They drank in silence for a bit. Rambo chanced his luck and shifted his legs so they were propped against the woman's stool, his right knee brushing against the top of her thigh. She didn't move. He was definitely in. Lovely. He checked on Greg for the first few minutes, then forgot about him. He was jammed into the TV and happy enough. That was the trouble with junkies. They lived in a dream world and nobody could help them. They had to help themselves. Rambo was going to help himself soon enough.

—I'm sorry about your bum getting bruised. I hope it was okay.

—Don't worry. It was worth it, even if you left me wanting at the end.

Rambo knew it was going to be a good night. She didn't seem that pissed either. He looked at her eyes to see if she was all there. She looked okay. Still, you never could tell. They chatted for a while and the woman told Rambo she was living round her sister's, with her brother-in-law and their three kids. That ruled her place out. He couldn't take her to his mum's flat, that just wouldn't do, and anyway, the old girl would ask what had happened to Greg. He looked over at the man in question and the silly sod was sitting there like a statue, crick in his neck, eyes fixed on the screen, listening to the programme, taking everything in. Rambo hated Coronation Street and EastEnders. What was the fucking difference? The same old pub scenes.

....

Men and women lined along pub bars talking shit. Wasting time when all they wanted was quick sex.

—You could make it up to me before I go home. I told my sister I'd be back by eight. Where are you staying? Have you got your own place?

Rambo broke the bad news but she didn't seem too bothered. She emptied her glass and looked at her watch, turned away from the bar and smiled.

—We could go outside if you like, as long as you don't hurt my bum again. Round by the garages. I'm not pissed this time, and neither are you, so I can get the full benefit.

Rambo couldn't believe his luck. Fair enough, if they were both pissed it would be understandable, but the night was still young and he was getting it on a plate. It was already turning into a freak evening, meeting Greg and the woman at the same time, so many years later, and Greg had just melted into the background he was so far into his own little dream world.

—I'll meet you round the back. Behind the garages on the other side of the car park. Don't be long.

He watched her arse cross the pub and go outside, then looked over towards Greg. Old Square Eyes. Fucking loser. Junky scum. He wasn't taking any chances with the woman. She said she was clean, but you couldn't believe anyone these days. He was living in a dangerous age when a harmless spot of in-and-out could result in a horrific, lingering death. He went for a piss and splashed out on some rubbers. There was no way he was getting stitched up by some smackhead.

The woman was waiting behind the garages as she'd promised, sitting on a broken wall. He positioned himself and they started kissing. The place stunk of stale piss and rotting vegetation. Not exactly classy, but then neither were the dustbins last time. He wasn't complaining. He soon had her tits out and her jeans

....

down round her ankles, and then she was slipping out of her shoes and taking her jeans right off. She folded them neatly and put them on the wall. She wasted no time getting Rambo out in the fresh air and he was surprised looking down to see what a hairy fucker she was. She needed a shave, but the smell was strong enough. Piss, rotting leaves and cunt oil. He felt like he was on one of those wildlife documentaries. The rutting season had started. And Rambo was star of the show.

—Do you remember those boys who came walking round the corner when we were doing it? They couldn't have been more than fifteen and you told them to fuck off. What did you call them?

—Peeping Toms. I'd forgotten about that. They ran off, but I still felt like they were there watching.

—You didn't stop, though, did you? Not till you'd come. They *were* watching, you know, because I could see them. I stuck my tongue out but it was dark so they couldn't have seen all that much.

Rambo didn't have a very clear memory of the evening. Just the odd highlight and slow-motion replay, an occasional frozen frame. He'd been hammered. More than that, it was like he was tripping. It had been dark and the junky slut didn't care. No shame. That's what smack did to you. It was disgusting.

—Stick it in me from behind. I'm ready now. I don't want to be late home. My sister's making a stew. It's my favourite and there's a good film on tonight. A classic John Wayne Western.

Fucking TV addicts everywhere. Worse than crack fiends. What was wrong with these people? When Rambo worked in the North Sea he'd made sure he had a good time when he got back on dry land. He'd seen enough television on the rigs to last a lifetime. He was sick of the shit they showed. It did nothing for

....

30

him. It shrivelled the brain and destroyed the soul. TV, satellite, video. It was all the same. A numbing disease destined to destroy humanity.

—Come on Rambo. Wait for me to turn round. I don't want my bum bruised again. And make sure you make it a bit better than last time. Try counting sheep and wait for me to get off as well.

Rambo felt his knob twitch with fear. He didn't like the formal tone of voice. Neither did he expect anything but gratitude. He couldn't hang around waiting for ever. She was leaning forward, forearms resting on the wall as she assumed the position. He thought he should search her. A line of detectives lining up waiting their turn. Kojak, Columbo, McCloud, even that cripple Ironside was there. Lurking in the undergrowth sucking lollipops, sucking cock in dirty raincoats and John Wayne cowboy hats, picking up freaks and shaving their heads. He shook his head. The sickness was spreading. She had a nice arse and he felt the old confidence return.

He was just about to get stuck in when he remembered the rubbers. Very clever. He opened the pack and rolled one on. He was fucking sharp and had to congratulate himself. There were no flies on Rambo. The break in action gave him a chance to look around. They were fairly well shielded by the garage and a tangle of bushes and rubbish, but if someone passed close by they'd be seen. It made him nervous, the thought that strangers could pry into his private affairs, zoom in and see his facial expressions. But what was the choice? Turn the woman down? He would take his chances. What could they do to him? But he felt like a crowd of pissheads were watching him in action, pushing past the detectives for a front-row seat, like he was a film star, a porn king, a soap opera celebrity. He

....

breathed in and concentrated. There was no way he was getting put off by a spark of unwanted imagination.

—Come on, what are you waiting for?

—All right, I'm on my way.

—Don't even think about sticking it up my bum either. Some weirdo tried that last week and he was so mean he didn't even do the groundwork first. Tried slamming it straight in. How's a girl supposed to enjoy that?

Rambo was pleased he'd remembered the rubber. Within thirty seconds the smell of burning rubber filled the air. Piss, rotting vegetation, love juice and now rubber. What a cocktail. He was aware he was in the open when he heard children's voices near by, and started shagging the junky subhuman faster. He wanted to get his pleasure and piss off.

—Come on. Quicker you bastard.

If this degenerate thought she was going to get an orgasm out of Rambo she was in for a surprise. He blew his beans in the rubber and pulled out. It felt strange on the end of his knob. He looked down. It was broken. The fucking thing had burst. He couldn't believe it. He thought of punctured veins and bone-dry arseholes, the curse of HIV.

—You could have kept going a bit longer. I was getting somewhere when you finished. Another five minutes, that's all I needed to be sure.

—Fuck that. The rubber broke.

—I'm on the pill. Don't worry about it.

She looked down at the split condom. There was a red and white solution covering his sagging penis, dripping over his balls to the top of his legs. She saw his mind ticking over as he put two and two together. He yanked the rubber off and threw it in among the broken branches and rusted cans.

—You're on. You never told me that. You're on.

. . . .

—So what? I'm just starting. I didn't know there was any blood yet. It's only a bit of blood sport.

—Let me see your arms?

—What?

—Let me see your arms?

—Why?

—I want to see if you're clean.

The woman rolled up her sleeves. Her arms were perfect. There weren't even any scars. He was confused. The one thing he remembered from that night six years ago were the puncture marks glowing in the dark like mutant fireflies.

—I thought you were a smackhead.

—Course not. I don't know where you got that from. You've been watching too many films. Too many police stories.

—You just said you'd cleaned yourself up. In the pub.

—I was mucking around. You were going on about junkies that night. You kept talking about it all the time like you were obsessed.

She soon had her jeans on and was tying the laces of her shoes. She looked at her watch. EastEnders was over and soon John Wayne would be killing Indians, Bad Guys and anyone else who stood in the way of the spread of civilisation. She wanted her stew before she settled down for the night, shook her head sadly and walked away, leaving Rambo leaning against the wall with his jeans pulled up but still undone. He stood there for a few minutes thinking. He was getting paranoid. Like he was being watched.

—You all right Rambo? Greg asked, when he went back in the pub.

Greg was laughing and shaking his head. Men were walking away smiling. Knowing smiles. Rambo needed a drink and turned towards the bar. Greg was quickly

....

on his feet, said it was his round, that just because he
didn't drink did Rambo think he wasn't going to buy
a round? There was a documentary about to start.
Lions in Africa. Baby lions and herds of wildebeest or
some such meat supply. It looked good. Better than
the fucking soap operas. Cunts standing at the bar
in the Queen Vic and Rovers. Fucking clowns the lot
of them. Nothing like real life. Didn't have a clue.

—There you go, Rambo. It was lager, wasn't it? I
don't pay much attention since I gave up the drink.
I can still get my round in though.

—What were you watching while I was gone? Was
it EastEnders or Coronation Street? We used to watch
them on the rigs. Nothing else to do. Just watched them
to kill time. It does your head in after a while.

—EastEnders.

—Life's not like that, though, is it?

—It was a blinder tonight. I'm surprised they put
it on so early. One of the regulars got shagged by an
outsider, this bloke back down from Scotland. They
didn't leave much to the imagination either. The whole
pub was into it. You know what it's like, they have to
get all the big issues in. Sex, drugs, AIDS. It had everything. The ratings will be good for that episode. The
whole country will have tuned in.

Rambo nodded and lifted the glass to his lips. Lovely.
A decent pint at last. Greg was almost animated. His
whole life had come to rely on what he saw on the
screen. The country was full of junkies. Rambo fucking
hated them. But Greg had sorted himself out.

—I just shafted that bird from six years ago.

—Yeah, I know.

—Corked her behind the garages. It's a coincidence
you were both here in the same place. Pure chance.

—There's no such thing as chance.

Rambo looked at Greg and wanted to grab hold of

....

him and shake some sense into his head. That's what drugs did to you. Fucked up your brain and gave you mad ideas. What happened to dignity and pride and restraint? You had to have standards. No such thing as chance? Of course there was. It was all that rubbish about butterflies flapping their wings in China, that's what Square Eyes was getting at, and the vibrations went right round the planet, and because of the butterfly some cunt's rubber split in London. It was insanity. Airy-fairy nonsense. No sense of reality.

—They closed the Pipemaker's and this is the only decent pub round here. She often comes in for a drink on her way home from work. It's the economy, not chance.

Rambo sat back and enjoyed his drink. Greg was opening up a bit now, but really wanted to watch the programme on lions. He was making a brave effort. There were some good aerial shots and Rambo wondered if they were shot from a plane or balloon. Maybe they used a satellite out in space. They used that kind of sophisticated technology for spying. It was magic that, dipping into people's lives. You couldn't even have a shag these days without getting caught on film. When the documentary was over Greg clapped his hands together and said that he had to get home. There was a good film on, a John Wayne classic, which he didn't want to miss. He didn't like staying out late these days. Not since he'd got his life cleaned up and kicked the chemicals.

—Is that bird I shagged a junky? Rambo asked as they got up to leave.

—Wouldn't have thought so. Might be, but nobody's ever told me, and I should know.

—I just remember her arms covered in burning punctures when we were behind Tesco's. It's the strongest

....

35

memory I have. That's why I wore a rubber tonight, but it split.

—Yeah, the whole pub cracked up laughing when that happened. They even had a Government AIDS warning on after the credits.

Greg looked a bit sheepish.

—I slipped you some acid that night. You kept going on about that woman, moaning about junkies and everything, repeating the rubbish they put on TV, self-righteous and full of shit. Sorry about that. It seemed like a laugh at the time. You deserved it.

Rambo put the empties on the bar and followed Greg outside. He didn't like the idea of appearing on national television during peak hours. What if his mum was watching? She wouldn't be impressed.

—What are you going to do now you're back? Greg asked, checking his watch. You going to try and find work here or go back on the rigs?

—There's nothing in Scotland, and I don't fancy coming back to live. There's no privacy in London. I'll be going somewhere new.

Greg nodded. Looked down the street.

—Maybe I'll see you before you go, Rambo. Give us a knock.

—Yeah. Look after yourself, Greg.

Greg turned and started walking away. He was a bit hunched, but he had always been like that, even as a kid. He wasn't a bad bloke really. Rambo called after him.

—Square Eyes.

Greg stopped and turned. He was grinning.

—Yeah?

—What film is it? I might watch it myself. You can't beat an old classic.

Beats on the Beach

LYNNE TILLMAN

There was shit everywhere, garbage and fat bodies and rotting hot dogs and I was disgusted on the beach. The scene was coming down around me and I stared at the ocean, melancholy and lonely, green and cool, and far away, way out there, was Europe and history and the ghosts of Baudelaire and Rimbaud and those very alive French girls—the green waves were their breasts rising and falling something like my cock when I'm horny, needy and angry as a dirty syringe, on those rocky nights of the soul. But not now, not today.

O inconstancy—i had to concentrate because of the shit on the beach, those straight surfer goons strutting around and kicking sand, and me, haggard, stretched tight like a drum over this mad existence, burned out, my whole body a night yellow white except for my left hand, the one I hang out the driver's window to feel the cool American breeze rush crazily over my American skin. Sometimes when I'm rolling along the highway of dreams, I let that hand lay on top of the roof of the car like I don't have a care in the world and my dog's next to me, grinning like an idiot, happy the way a dog can be, his short hind legs on the back seat, his head resting next to my shoulder, content as I drive along. My dog, the one I left with Riva, Riva the dancer, she just kissed me good-bye and whispered—Later, baby.

I shot a glance at Allen who was smiling in his strange

inward cerebral way because he was thinking of something bigger that wasn't on the beach.

—What a chick Riva was, man. She'd make your hair curl, if you had any.

The Beanbag—that's what we called him—turned to me and muttered, Leave it alone, Fast Jack, suck on your own dick for a while. Don't get angry, my man, I answered, and I swore I would love him until the day I die which might be tomorrow because tomorrow always comes and how many tomorrows does any man have.

I dug him, I did. Allen was America's bearded idealist, hopeful and scared but eager and ready to face Life when it happened, a true poet, the kind I was striving to be, because I wanted to live the Life with everything in me, to be Real in the face of phony gutless pathetic humanity, the human subspecies, but here on the beach Allen looked weird, a skinny New York intellectual on the sand near the ocean, all pale and frail and gray around the edges from long nights in clubs talking the smart hip talk to other hipsters of the future, and sometimes I thought about him, us, because if you split us open, you'd find bars, bottles, tables and chairs, but in him, there would be books and bookcases, addresses, a card catalogue and eyeglasses, BECAUSE he—WE—we're the poets of airless, smoky rooms, word-makers in the hidden factories of the American spirit.

Life is shit and you have to be ready to give it up, ride off on an endless road to nowhere, disappear in a hotel room so ugly even Wild Bill would snicker at the cliché, his eyes half-closed while he's nodding, high on some heavy shit that gives him the vision he needs to see right through the merciless nothing of everything. Allen wanted me, I didn't want him, I wanted someone,

Wild Bill hungered for Allen, they were making the scene.

—Hey, Beanbag, rub a little of that on my back.

Allen looked up kind of stunned like he was just born and I had to laugh at his beautiful ignorance and his innocence. He didn't even know he was on the beach, his head in a book while I was watching some cute little girls walking by and thinking how it was in high school and how my mom loved me, but I don't want to think about that, about the past, how I only had orgasms when I fantasized about her leaving me, and it's sad for eternity. Allen rubbed some lotion on my white back which was turning color under the wild rays of the heartless sun. The imperturbable ocean rolling and roiling let me forget for a minute the people somewhere else toiling and sweating, working their insides out—for what, for a buck, for what else in this stinking world, and those politicians with their platitudinous cant, it makes me sick, even on the beach, because which way to turn, to look. I gotta look so I do.

Out of nowhere the Marvelous Magician from Hell comes toward us, Wild Bill wearing a djellabah that covers him like a tent so no one can see the frozen rivers that are his veins and the scabrous body he calls home. I've seen that expression on Wild Bill's face before, when he's thinking of what he's lost or the Midwest or history, a so-what, an Is This All There Is? Wild Bill lights a cigarette with a match that appears like he did out of nowhere—the ether—and he sits down on the blanket next to the Beanbag, who's dousing his own white hairy body with suntan lotion.

Wild Bill snorts—That crummy lotion your cover story, Allen, you think the agents of the Polyester Poison Sunboy won't find you here? Won't get you? Ah, relax, Beanbag, the Black Meat Mamas don't want your skinny ass. I've got something in my pocket that'll melt you into just so many lumps of carcinogenic plasm.

The Beanbag and Wild Bill kissed a long time and I lost myself in them, their sticky bodies, their wet mouths merged into one enormous American soul kiss, it was gorgeous. Boom. And I remembered that little blonde girl in Cincinnati and how I loved her but couldn't stay, because I never can, can't stay in love with one, because I'm in love with the One and All, but then I thought about poetry and prose, how the word could illuminate if I could just find it, the right word. Like Wild Bill who can—he writes and there's blood on the page, he spills his guts and I don't mean metaphorically, I'm talking about real blood on the page, so thick and dark that Allen can't read the words underneath without scraping it off and dumping it on the floor.

The sun was beating down and later Allen was goofing to Wild Bill about another poet, Bra Man—this cat, the Beanbag was wailing now, thinks panty raids are bourgeois, that's why he steals chicks' boobie traps—that's what he calls them—and we laughed a long time, but really Allen wanted to be in Paris or Tangier, away from the indifferent ugliness of America, but when I leave I feel homesick, homesick in my depths, and I just don't know.

I get so lonely, even here on the beach, and Wild Bill says, Fast Jack, grab yourself a beer and watch some TV, the way you always do and have, and always will, and Bill is right, that's what I do, that's what I did, I can't change, I am what I am, a man. And that's all there is, that and the beach, the bigger than life ocean and the grains of sand, they're like miracles, wonders in this Mongolia of existence. It gets me, really, this beauty, and it keeps me hooked to Life.

But watching Wild Bill and the Beanbag I knew I

....

was really alone, with them but not with them, I never did dig men, not that way, because that's not my scene, so I was with them and not with them, and they understood, and it was cool, and I would move on, leave, the way I always leave, I have to leave everybody.

I popped open another beer and patted my stomach which was getting bigger every day. Allen says I look like I'm carrying his baby and, you know, I'd dig that, to give birth to his baby, to put something in the world, not just words—well, words too because they're important, poetry is the Truth—but a baby who'd grow up and drive across the country, his hand lying on the roof of the car, the American breeze blowing, my boy who'd say one day—Fast Jack was my dad and he was cool.

Not Quite Roman Polanski

BARRY GRAHAM

for Irvine Welsh
'A breath of fresh air even stinking of the bevvy he made all teenage weather seem heavy'

– Paul Reekie

Scumbo met her at the Venue. It was a Friday night in November and he hadn't really wanted to go out. He had a running cold and wasn't feeling sociable anyway. But he was friendly with one of the three bands who were playing and he'd promised to be there. And at least the Venue was warm, which was more than could be said about his flat.

He walked across town to the Venue. The night was dry and frozen. He hadn't eaten much that day, and by the time he got there he was weak and shaky. It was about nine o'clock – half an hour before the gig was due to start – so he went to the Cooler, in the basement of the Venue, for a drink.

The place was nearly empty. It opened till three in the morning, so most of the clientele didn't show up till after midnight, when most other pubs had shut.

Scumbo drank a whisky and watched two fat bikers playing pool. Three girls came in. They were all worth a shag, but they were too young and giggly for him to bother with. He drank another whisky, felt better and went upstairs to the Venue.

The first band was already on stage. Scumbo had heard they were brilliant. Maybe they were, but not at music. The front man had spent too much time sitting alone in his bedroom. Scumbo went to the bar and got another drink.

It was quite busy, and more people were arriving. Scumbo knew some of them, and they stood at the back and traded small talk.

Then the second band came on, the one his friends were in. The crowd warmed up. The band was quite raucous, and some people down at the front started to dance.

Scumbo didn't. He was feeling feverish. He had on a T-shirt, a heavy lumberjack shirt, an even heavier sweater, a tartan scarf, a ski cap and a biker's jacket. The heat and the whisky were bringing him near boiling point. He felt like he might faint.

He took off the jacket and sweater and sat down on the floor. He felt like shit. Through the darkness and dry ice, several figures waved to him. He waved back without being able to see who they were.

Somebody squatted down next to him. It was his friend Spam. He was speeding.

'*Never saw you sitting here*,' he bawled in Scumbo's ear. '*Nearly tripped over you.*'

Scumbo smiled morosely.

'*You okay?*' Spam enquired at a thousand decibels.

'*Yeah. I'm fine*,' Scumbo yelled with as much energy as he could muster.

'*I'm out my face*,' Spam informed him. Scumbo was less than astounded. Spam was usually out of his face; it was only the specific drug that varied. He'd disapproved when Scumbo had sworn off drugs following an embarrassing incident a few months earlier, when he'd

....

become convinced that the barman in the Cooler was Jesus and had then tried to make everybody else in the pub aware of the fact.

'*Want some Lou Reed?*' asked Spam.

'*Nah. I'll stick to the bevvy.*'

'*Fucking Mormon.*'

Spam did some more speed, then got up and started dancing. Scumbo lost sight of him. The band finished and there was a break before the headline band came on. Scumbo went to the bar and drank a pint of water. Then he got another whisky.

The three young girls he'd seen in the Cooler were standing in the queue for drinks. As Scumbo walked past, one of them stopped him with a nudge.

'Have I seen you busking in Rose Street?'

'Yeah,' he said. 'Now and again.'

She turned to her friends. 'See! I *told* you!' For some reason they found this hysterically funny. Scumbo made his escape.

He wasn't keen on the headline band. He watched them for a while, then found the dressing room where his friends, gig accomplished, were busy getting wasted.

It was just a crummy little room with chairs and a mirror, which all the bands shared. His friends the Surrogate Fathers were skinning up joints and drinking beer. There were six-packs of beer all over the floor, maybe provided by the Venue.

Scumbo offered the musos the usual congratulations, then told them he had to head off. They said they'd be offended if he left their gig sober. He stayed and, out of politeness, washed down a lump of their dope with a few cans of their beer.

The headline band returned to the room and joined in the festivities. Scumbo decided to get out of there. The dope was making him horny. He was even starting to fancy Morticia, the lead singer with the Surrogate

....

Fathers. Since her boyfriend was a friend of Scumbo's and also played in the band, this wasn't an ideal state of affairs.

He left without saying anything and went to the Cooler. It was jumping, and more people were coming in as other places closed. As usual, there was a general air of menace, but no actual trouble. Scumbo had a theory about why you so rarely saw any fights in the Cooler: it being such a mental place, he reckoned everybody who went there probably assumed that everybody else must be as mental as they were, or they wouldn't be there. So nobody wanted to start anything.

Scumbo went to the bar and got two whiskies, so he wouldn't have to queue when he'd finished the first one. Then he went looking for a seat.

He couldn't find one, but he saw Spam sitting at a table with some people he knew slightly. He went over, put his drinks down on the table and sat on Spam's knee.

'*Want some Bob Hope?*' Spam yelled over the Rod Stewart music from the jukebox.

'*Naw, I've just had some.*'

'*My boy!*' Spam slapped him on the back. '*Where'd you get it?*'

'*Morticia gave me it.*'

'*There's a party later on. Want to go?*' Spam was hoarse from shouting.

'*Whose?*'

'*Don't know. It's in Newington.*'

'*Will there be any fanny?*'

Spam sniffed. '*Do you really expect me to indulge in such sexism?*' The self-righteous tone was lost at such volume. '*I'm sure human beings of either gender will be present. Don't get excited, though,*' he added. '*I've never got laid at a party.*'

Scumbo laughed. Spam couldn't get laid if you sent

....

him to a brothel with a blank cheque. He had his Lou
Reed and his Bob Hope, but never his Nat King Cole.

The two whiskies went the way of all flesh, and
Scumbo went back to the bar. While he was waiting,
somebody nudged him. It was the girl he'd seen earlier,
who'd asked if he busked in Rose Street.

She smiled and said something he couldn't hear. He
leaned close to her (he could smell her deodorant) and
asked if she'd like a drink. She indicated that she
already had one. Thank fuck, thought Scumbo. He'd
hardly any money left as it was.

He got a whisky and beckoned to the girl to follow
him, wondering if she would. She did. They went and
sat on the floor just outside the door, where you could
at least hear yourself speak.

Her name was Hilary. She wasn't bad looking, small
and a bit on the plump side, with blonde bobbed hair
and a nice smile. Scumbo asked if she had a job and
she said she was still at school.

'How old are you?'

'Sixteen.'

'Oh.'

'What about you?'

'Twenty-six.'

'Does it bother you that I'm sixteen?'

Scumbo kissed her on the mouth, quite lightly. She
grinned at him. 'Does it bother you that I'm sixteen?'
she asked again.

He gave her a longer kiss, then moved to her neck.
She lost her jocularity and began breathing heavily.
When he went back to her mouth she kissed him slowly
and ferociously, sucking on his teeth and lips.

They kissed like that for quite a while. Scumbo
shoved against her, then had to stop doing that when
he got worried that he might actually come. Typical.
He should have had a wank before he left home.

....

Finally, Scumbo said, 'There's supposed to be a party somewhere. Want to go?'

She shook her head.

'Me neither. Fancy going back to my flat?'

'Yeah, but I can't. My mum'll crack up if I'm out all night. And my friends might tell her I was with a guy.'

Scumbo remembered the giggling of her friends and had to agree they might not be paragons of discretion. 'Okay,' he said. 'What about tomorrow night?'

She nodded. 'Phone me tomorrow. Or I can phone you.' They swapped numbers, then she rounded up her colleagues from the kindergarten and left with them.

Scumbo went to the party with Spam. It was a miserable affair, full of student members of some left-wing organisation. Spam let some girl lecture him on the shortcomings of democracy on the off-chance that she might shag him at the end of the night. Scumbo decided that the end of the night had already arrived. He walked to his flat in Bruntsfield.

He drank a pint of water and went to bed. He thought about Hilary and had a quick wank, then a nice slow one about fifteen minutes later.

Then he slept.

He was wakened by the phone ringing at noon. He ignored it until his flatmate banged on his bedroom door. He put on his dressing gown and went out to the hall. He felt terminal.

'Hi. It's Hilary.' She didn't sound any better than he felt.

'Hi, how're you doing?'

'I can't see you tonight. My mum won't let me go out.'

'How come?'

'She's pissed off because I've got a hangover.'

Scumbo laughed. 'So when will you get out to play?'

....

'Give me your address. I'll bunk off school and come and see you on Monday.'

'Okay. Great.' He gave her the address.

'I'd better tell you,' she added. 'It's my first time.'

He wanked himself thin over the weekend. But by Monday morning his excitement was diluted with paranoia.

What if she'd lied about her age? What if she was under sixteen? It was hard to tell sometimes.

She arrived just after ten o'clock. Scumbo was in his dressing gown, having just got up and had some coffee. When he opened the door, she was standing there in her school uniform.

That did it. He began seeing newspaper reports of his trial and conviction. *Find out her age. What if she is only fifteen? It's amazing the difference a year makes. If she's fifteen you're a child molester. If she's sixteen you're a lucky bastard.*

'Hilary – Listen – ' *This is surreal.* 'Have you got any ID?'

'What d'you mean, ID? What for?' They went into his bedroom and closed the door.

'Well – ' *Just tell her.* 'To prove your age.'

She looked at him. 'Are you serious? Bouncers and barmen don't even ask me to prove my age.'

'Bouncers and barmen aren't going to get locked up if they get your age wrong. I'm a law-abiding citizen.'

'Jesus. You're worse than my mum.' She showed him her bus pass. He looked at the date of birth and did some mental arithmetic: she would be seventeen in three weeks' time.

'Okay,' he said and started to kiss her, but she was annoyed and unresponsive. That soon changed, when he started stroking her tits through her white blouse

....

48

and bra, as he teased her nipples she closed her eyes and her breathing got heavy.

They lay on the bed and kissed, tongues fucking mouths. The room was cold, so they got under the duvet before undressing. Scumbo put his hand up her skirt. The look and feel of her navy blue tights did something to him he couldn't understand.

He slipped off his dressing gown and helped her off with her clothes. Her body was all right; she had some puppy fat that would disappear in the next year or two.

Scumbo could see she was nervous. He went down on her and she came almost as soon as his tongue touched her. She came again soon after, as Scumbo sucked on her clit and moved his index finger in and out of her.

She lost her nervousness after they'd fucked properly. She'd been afraid it would hurt, but it didn't. But she found she couldn't come with his cock inside her. That was no problem, though. He fingered her and licked her out a few times more, and each time she came like a kettle boiling.

They fucked twice more, and she wanked him once. She didn't go down on him and he didn't ask her to. Time enough for that.

She got dressed in a hurry at three o'clock. 'I'll have to get back over to the school. My dad's picking me up in his car.' She rummaged in her holdall and found a brown paper bag. She dropped it on the bed. 'That's my lunch. I'd better leave it here. My mum searches my bag, though she says she doesn't. If she finds it she'll give me a hard time about not eating.'

Scumbo just lay in bed and smiled and nodded. He was tired and dehydrated and hungry.

Hilary kissed him. 'Right, I'll have to run. See you on Friday.' She left.

Scumbo didn't see her out. He didn't want to get up

....

until he really had to. The room was cold and the bed was warm. He could see his breath. He opened Hilary's paper bag. A cheese sandwich, a packet of prawn cocktail crisps and a carton of chocolate-flavoured milk. It brought back memories. Best days of your life. Yeah.

Scumbo devoured the sandwich and crisps, then washed it down with the chocolate milk. It was starting to get dark outside. Hilary would be back on Friday, taking another day off school. He hoped her education wouldn't suffer too badly.

– November 1993

Where the Railway Meets the River

GARY INDIANA

The next thing, Robert told me, was an acting job Paul took on a shoot in Malta, and after that he traveled around to Paris and London, looking up friends, avoiding other friends. Valentina was left with the chore of notifying the other friends about Ray's death. She did this in rather a perfunctory manner, despite the aggrieved voice she used on the phone: she told everyone about Paul going to Malta and his being too upset to talk and said he would get in contact eventually. A long time passed, Robert said, with no word from Paul whatsoever. Meanwhile, Robert heard that Chris had died, carried off with remarkable speed by pneumonia.

One day, apparently by chance, Paul did pick up the telephone when Robert rang the flat, and before he could make an excuse to hang up Robert insisted on meeting him somewhere. They met in the café on the ground floor of Paul's building. Paul looked like he'd been sleeping in his clothes, distracted, pallid. He chain-smoked and ordered coffee after coffee. He fidgeted with a paper napkin and tore it into tiny pieces. Terrible overwrought silences stretched between bursts of disconnected chatter. Paul groped for words, ideas. His hands gestured strangely, as if fingering an elusive ectoplasm. He talked of going to America. He mentioned hooking up again with Alex to make another movie. He said he had an idea for a comedy set in India, about two servants running a house owned by Greta Garbo.

'Guests arrive, wanting to see Miss G., and the servants make it impossible for them.'

He said he'd had Ray cremated. The ashes were in a little urn, he said a stainless steel urn that looked like a cocktail shaker. When spring came, he said, he and Valentina would fly with the ashes to Australia, stopping here and there along the way to visit friends.

Paul rubbed his unshaven jaw with his dirty fingers. Robert told him the important thing was to work through his grief and somehow go on with life. Paul nodded agreement but without conviction. Lighting another cigarette, wiping his smeary glasses on a napkin, he glanced around the crowded café and said he was deathly tired of life and of looking at the same streets, the same restaurants, the same dreadful people and anywhere else was worse, or the same, a complete trap. Paul remarked, according to Robert, if you begin to take an interest, pretend that tomorrow begins a new day, then you've really had it. Robert saw that Paul struggled to inhabit the moment rather than cave in under awful feelings. Paul took a little pill, he noticed. A while later Paul said, 'Do you know, after all these years I at last made a little pilgrimage to Dachau?'

This recent memory seemed to focus his thoughts. As he described the trip, he became more himself. Paul said that he had arranged a little trip to Munich for Michael Simard – 'who is working as a rent boy,' Paul told Robert – offering to pay him something like a thousand dollars for the weekend. But before Michael Simard arrived, Paul looked up Billy Sauberman and copped several doses of Mickey Mouse blotter acid. He sent Valentina away (she was half living in the apartment by then) and prepared himself for a

....

52

weekend of heavy sex. He had an idea that had come to him, Robert said, as most of Paul's ideas came – that is to say, marching in heavy boots through his brainpan – and when he left for the airport he took the acid along with him.

Michael Simard looked even more like a GQ layout, having pumped himself relentlessly at the Chelsea Gym, and stepped off the seven-hour flight flawlessly groomed, in a green trench coat, black hair slicked back in a fashionable ponytail, the composed beauty of his face impassive as an executioner.

'Welcome to Germany.'

'It's been quite a long time, hasn't it?'

'Here, darling, put this under your tongue.'

As they drove on the autobahn, Michael talked. He talked about his job. He now serviced many famous people, and they all had little kinks.

'Many clients?'

'A lot of regular clients. Some days I do a lot, sometimes only one or two a week.'

'How many have you ever done in one night?'

'Oh, I don't know, three or four; if it starts early in the day, it could be as many as six.'

'And you spend an hour with each one?'

'An hour, or sometimes less, sometimes a little longer.'

'When you do so many, how do you manage to get a hard-on each time?'

'Well, the best thing is if you don't have to come. If someone sucks me I can usually manage a boner.'

'But then it goes limp when you try to fuck them?'

'Very rarely. You get used to the condom.'

'Do you advertise in the gay papers? Or just go to hustler bars?'

'If clients drop off, I run an ad. I mean, look, Paul, this isn't my vocation or anything. But it's good to

....

make a thousand dollars in a couple days, it makes you feel you have a stake in the economy.'

The padded steering wheel beneath Paul's fingers began to exhibit an organic tension, like the evenly muscled flesh of a boa constrictor. They talked about a famous murder case.

'I told him,' Michael was saying. 'I said, I know Andrew, I've done Andrew. He does enjoy piss, he does get into whipping. But no way would he have shot that Norwegian kid . . .'

The leafless branches overhanging the road were faintly haloed in Freon blue and green against a dense, lavender-gray cloud bank, as if they'd been dipped in water and laid against pillows of litmus paper.

'But they say the other guy shot him,' Paul said. 'While Andrew screwed him.'

The clouds sparkled with pink energy. They churned into blocky shapes of crabs and dolphins. Michael's American voice reached him in scratchy wriggles of sound he could barely make sense of. Paul clenched his jaw to keep the road focused.

'I know the Filipino,' Michael said. 'His father works for the UN. He's a shit queen.'

'The Filipino's father is a shit queen?'

'No, the kid, the kid. Ties you down, shits in your mouth. I don't get into it at either end unless somebody's really special, and that kid isn't. Andrew on the other hand likes to give pain, he likes to humiliate, but he knows where the limits are. It wouldn't surprise me if the Filipino snorted too much Coke and went out of control.'

Light traffic on the motorway consisted of noisy motes of chrome, gusts of exhaust, salt-crusted car windows. Indistinct faces framed in tinted windows. Paul moved his hand across the foamy ridges of the seat, over the firm casing of Michael's trouser leg,

. . . .

lodged between Michael's thighs. Michael shifted on his spine, thrusting his crotch closer. As Paul fondled his heavy penis through the fabric, Michael's expression remained bright, neutral. His brittle fingers, lower joints sprouting vivid black hairs, brushed the back of Paul's hand. The pyramidal roofs of the Dachau guardhouses drifted into view.

'Could you do that?' Paul wanted to know. 'Just shoot somebody?'

'Me? Fuck, man, not my scene.'

'If somebody made it sexy for you? And the guy wore a leather hood over his face?'

'Hey, I don't believe in that shit.'

Paul steered the car into the parking area. 'What if there were no consequences? If you could absolutely get away with it?'

Michael thought about it and smiled.

'Don't put ideas in my head.'

There were five other cars in the lot, where rain from earlier in the day had puddled and begun to freeze. The cold surprised him as they got out. The drug danced on his nerve ends. His teeth clattered uncontrollably. Michael hopped eagerly on the pavement, vapor streaming from his nostrils. They walked along the slick path, crunching parchment sheets of ice, over a thicket of spidery plane-tree branches reflected in splotches of congealing water. Ahead was a sliding gate, half-open, maple branches entangled in loops of accordion wire. On the inner grounds, small groups of visitors walked along the edges of a concrete embankment, separated from the flat gravel walk facing the entrance by a ditch and a barbed-wire fence.

The fence was strung between concrete pylons. On the side of each pylon a metal-shaded floodlamp was trained on the rock slope and the concrete ditch. Hooked iron rods poked from the tops of the pylons, supporting the top strand of barbed wire. Across the ditch at the edge of the slope, a margin of grass massed in electric-green profusion.

The tourists moved around the corner of a recon-structed barracks. Paul forced himself to walk in that direction. His innards vibrated. He touched Michael's fingers. He thought he felt Michael's fingerprints, hair-thin ridges of identity merging with his own. The vibration in his body was overwhelmingly pleasant and a little sickening. He felt colors on his skin, mauve and yellow on his arms, crawling over his chest. Panels of ultraviolet light jumped through the air. Looking at Michael, he saw blood seeping from the soft parts of his skull. The air glued a breath of sap and decaying leaves to his nostrils.

Three tourist groups ranged irregularly between the ghost spaces of the barracks that had been razed after the war. Their figures wobbled in and out of sight, at times merging with trees and earth. Michael's face became a collection of squirming sea life, minnows and smelts and crayfish, pulsing under a cellophane skin. The fish mutated into parts of birds, leaves, vegetable roots. The pale yellow sweater under Michael's trench coat cupped his chin, holding the bits and pieces together, preventing his skull from snapping apart and disgorging his brain. Reptile lips slithered in worm motion. The nose sucked air into red cankered lungs that billowed under layers of flesh and fabric. As they reached the barracks, Paul devised a little mantra to organize the chaos in front of his eyes. Not so bad, not so bad, he whispered. Not so bad.

The fact that it wasn't so bad rubbed at his brain. The building resembled a subway car, the insides sanit-ized and solemn as a Lutheran chapel. A grid of bunks looked like vegetable bins. Here they slept. He looked for brain matter and shredded convict uniforms in the

....

pinewood architecture of precise diagonals, calibrated shadows, a place as lacking in horror as Heidegger's cottage in Todtnauberg.

Something yelled inside him that he didn't want to know about. He and Michael entered a reconstructed washroom. Paul later told Robert that at this point he recalled an account of Auschwitz-Birkenau about a trench so fetid with blood and maggots and corpses that prisoners, faced with the prospect of cleaning it out, preferred to be shot. Here all was clean. Two massive metal washstand saucers, mounted on pedestals pierced by fat hydraulic pipes, caught dull light from four contiguous windows in the far wall. The washstands and windows were insanely symmetrical: 'like everything,' Paul later told Robert, 'in this roaring disease of a country.' A thought danced unavoidably into his brain, announcing itself as the terrible secret of Dachau: 'This is kitsch.'

He felt phlegmy tar from a million cigarettes cling to the soft lobes of his lungs. He scanned Michael's face, which was growing a crust of weariness from travel and spectral dabs here and there from thousands of Jewish ghosts. But the fastidious room had never contained any victims, some professional atrocity memorialist had supervised its reconstruction. The ghosts had seeped into the ground, the air. At the end of the room a door led to a lavatory with eight ceramic toilet basins lining one wall, symmetrical, lidless, the repeated form suggesting a mold for plaster casts of the human face. Paul imagined millions of human faces gazing up out of a million toilet bowls.

Grimy bands of magenta and blue vibrated in the air like bands of exhausted confetti. Paul summoned images of pissing and shitting prisoners, heads shaved, forearms tattooed, emaciated, haggard, walking dead. But the pictures crumbled, leaving the single brittle

....

image of an artwork for mass guilt. Not stark, but 'stark', not moving, but 'moving', like everything arranged to stir the dead conscience of the world. And all the dead abandoned by God seemed doubly abandoned by the implacable transformation of emotions into kitsch.

Michael's skin was becoming translucent. He would soon turn to stone, Paul thought, to mica, or devolve into a poisonous green lizard, black tongue flicking, or a great smelly cheese oozing oily moisture. They said nothing. They sensed when to move from the shifting quality of the silence.

Outside, a concourse lined with skeletal poplars ran the length of the former concentration camp. The sites of vanished barracks were marked off with stubby plywood borders. The earth inside them was raised, mulched with debris. Their shoes crunched on the gravel. A rift in the clouds revealed a streak of liquid turquoise. A band of Scotch pines and pin oaks fluttered like a feather boa draped across the horizon. Michael asked hoarsely:

'Did you eat today?'

'Don't tell me this is making you hungry.'

'I had something on the plane.'

'I would like a cigarette, though.'

Paul laughed and shivered and Michael laughed at his shivering. The laughter fell like an act of vandalism in the freezing gloom.

'This is where they killed people?'

'It was more like a work camp. The big killing places were in Poland mostly.'

Michael shook his head. 'I should know more about that stuff than I do. I always meant to read up on it.'

The path continued over a canal to the crematorium. They paused on a blunt narrow bridge and stared at a dense growth of birches and pines along the canal bank.

....

Strands of barbed wire extended above the bridge railing. The silver-black water, stirred by a strong current, flowed over the knotted roots of dying locust trees. Michael's expression was intense yet unreadable. He remains completely mysterious, Paul later told Robert, as if he had no real existence as a person, but were only an ideal of beauty.

When they came within sight of the main crematorium, a somber parade of foreigners was marching away from it, heading back over the bridge. The area appeared deserted now. The acid would peak very soon, Paul realized. The bricks of the crematorium breathed and expanded and shrank back into their grooves. Paul marched close to the wall, running his fingertips over the bricks. Michael trailed him, hands stuffed into his trench coat. Paul felt the grass slither underfoot. He lost his place in the story. Once upon a time, there was a little boy whose mother lived with him all alone in a contaminated forest. He froze and threw his back against the wall and stared at the chill sky. In his head he spoke to the emptiness behind the clouds and wished for a primal moment, as a strong wind surged up from the south. Once upon a time, there was a mother and a boy.

They walked across the rolling lawn behind the crematorium. Once upon a time, they went to the witch's house. And there was the wolf who had eaten the old grandmother, but they left a trail of crumbs. And then a sparrow came and ate the crumbs. Only the prince can find the pearl in the bottom of the sea, only his lips can wake the princess. They approached the smaller crematorium, near a trimmed bare arbor vitae hedge. *Thank God that no one knows my name is really Rumpelstiltskin.*

....

It was a plain garage-like building, Paul later told Robert, with a peaked tile roof, its walls brushed by frostbitten quince bushes. We're coming to the end, Paul thought. His mind jumped its tracks again. He was twelve years old, with his friend from school, a boy named Peter Seitz, fetching a rake from the potting shed where the dust held the sharp smell of fertilizer. They piled leaves from the elm tree, raked bales of leaves into tall mounds and ran skidding into them and touched, he touched him through the crackling leaves, later the leaves were burned. Smoke on frosty afternoons gone long ago today tomorrow and then gone for ever.

'You can still get a boner?' Paul asked.

'Are you kidding?' Michael said. 'I *have* one.'

A wreath affixed to the oven. Bare cement floor. Two metal grates set into it at the base of two brick kilns flanking the main oven. It was never used, he recalled. Fire is not your friend, he thought. The middle oven resembled an altar: two arched chambers, like cartoon eyelids, oxidized doors yawning open on corroded hinges. Bring me your poor, your tired. Small rectangular openings below. Chimney pipes ran from the crest of the brickwork into the roof. There was an empty space behind the incineration area, barred by a wrought-iron gate.

And then, Paul later told Robert, as everything unfolded, the scattered lyrics of a dozen sappy songs whistled through his brain, kitsch for the kitsch-hearted, he said. *If ever I would leave you*, Paul climbed over the gate, *it wouldn't be in the summer*. A dank, empty space between the ovens and the wall. *There's a place for us, somewhere a place for us.* Michael swung his leg over the railing. *Pardon me boy, is this the Chattanooga Choo-choo?* They wouldn't be invisible from the main room, but it did provide a modicum of privacy.

....

This is a good space, Paul thought. A wasted space. A space that would have been used for stacking corpses, clean as a German floor. *Take one fresh and tender kiss.* He unbuttoned his shirt, shucking off his parka. A drizzle of colored atoms congealed in the chamber. *Add one stolen night of bliss.* One boy, one girl, functioning incinerator, memories are made of this.

Orange light exploded in the room. Memories. War photographs. Soldiers caked with mud. Rotted boots. Smell of carbolic acid, cinders speckling the air. He sank his fingers into Michael's face. It came apart in soggy clumps of fat, bloody muck plopped onto butcher paper. Squids in a metal bin. Jagged hole opening. Veins stitched across a sticky membrane that covered wet fragments of bone. Inside the blue hole, the skinned head of a ferret. Alien life form sucking gristle from the walls of the cavity. Blue fingers wrestled off Michael's clothes. The sweater came away with a gout of hair and scalp attached.

Green vapor and the smell of disinfectant swirled from the ovens. Red pinpoints strobed in the billowing fog. Michael pulled off his shoes. He slid off his belt. Flesh melted from Paul's body as he shed his clothes. Sirens in the camp. Boots thudding over frozen earth near the perimeter fence. Bursts of submachine-gun fire.

The crematorium shook with the concussion of an antiaircraft barrage. Fleshless fingers tugged off Michael's jockstrap. Paul gripped Michael's inflamed penis. *There's no business like show business, like no business I know.* Their torsos collided. Skeletons raked through soft flesh. *Everything about it is appealing!* Their ribs fused. *Blue moon.* Paul pulled at Michael's hair and unfastened the ponytail. *You saw me standing alone.* His eyes. His throat. Michael shoved him against the oven. His tongue darted into the hole between Paul's lips. I want you. I need you. Paul's teeth fastened

....

to the slimy gland. *Am I blue? Am I blue?* Blood, salt and thick, coursed into his throat. He felt the armature of Michael's body convulse. *Do you know how to pony? like bony maroney?* Michael flipped him around, smashing Paul's chest into the wall.

Paul's eardrums fluttered as the sirens rose again. *It goes like this it goes like this.* Paul flattened his hands against the spackled cement. He bent forward with his legs spread. *Up there, there is a sea*, Michael crouched behind him digging fingers into Paul's hips. He lubricated the anus with his bleeding tongue. *St Louis woman, with all your diamond rings, drag that man around by your apron strings.* Michael dropped one hand to jerk himself off. Green smoke rose between their bodies in the blue crematorium. *If it weren't for powder and all that store-bought hair.* Paul heard the troops marching like thunder, past the incinerators, motorcycles revving up, exhaust furrowing the highway yards away. *I've got you under my skin.* The flower of Abyssinia was opening. The sky was raging. The Lord is my shepherd, I shall not want. Michael's spit-wet member slid into the opening. He maketh me to lie down in green pastures. The hole opened like the Red Sea. He leadeth me beside the still waters. *Fuck my hole, Mr Death.* He restoreth my soul. Arteries. *You do something to me.* Scent of rectal mucus. Faint nauseating tang of roasted flesh. Yea, though I walk through the valley of the shadow of death, I will fear no evil for thou art with me. Michael's arms wrapped around him. His nipples were changing color. The limbs of a preying mantis encircled him.

Slice me up. The tongue bleeds over his shoulder. His organ is wet. His balls. The rectum gyrates around the stone-hard penis. In between. Two mineral beings freeze in the bleak diorama. The bodies turn to stone as pictures of skyrockets pinwheels flaming cities flash.

....

Phosphenes. Anemones palpitating under the cement floor. *Kiss me feel me kill me.* Paul flattened himself against the oven. He merged with the oven. They locked like dogs. The cock inside him spurted a cold acrid kerosene odor that permeated the room. They staggered away from the ovens locked together and collapsed after a grotesque waltz. Paul's face hit the floor. Michael's hips continued shaking. Fucking him face down, Michael swept the floor with his arms, grabbing up socks and underwear and jamming them under Paul's face. *Smell me.* His smooth buttocks translucent globes in a Bosch painting. Paul's come spurted on the cement. *What God has joined together.* Michael pulled out of him. He pushed Paul over on his back and stood over him, squatting over his face. He pumped his cock while the crematorium echoed his heavy breathing, gasped as he released a jet of opalescent semen, splattering Paul's eyelids. He squeezed the last drops of come into Paul's open mouth and uttered a cry of bewildered ecstasy.

The cold woke him, twitching, a pain in his side bringing the room back together. Pale light from a high window. Veins and bubbles in the wall plaster. They dressed with heavy, awkward movements, breath forming weak trails of varicolored vapor. Over the gate. The touch of metal on his palms sent a sharp metallic taste to his mouth. He watched the grim architecture settle into an old picture frame. Michael glazed over, wrapping himself in his coat with crisp, methodical movements. Paul felt for a marking pen he had in his jacket and wrote HIV on the glass door of the oven.

After they crossed the funereal esplanade of withered trees and entered the parking lot, Michael made a troubled face as if he expected something to come and punish him. Then he began to laugh. As Paul later told Robert, it was just another weird scene.

....

Heavy Petting

(for Tiny and Twinkle)

....

BRIDGET O'CONNOR

I come from a long line of pet deaths. Bunny and
Clyde ... Tiny and Twinkle. Sid and Nancy. Mungo ...

But it's Godfrey who haunts me.

At night, when the cistern gurgles, it's like he's back
with a splash.

Majella hooped him at a fairground and brought him
home, dangling from her thumb, gulping mist in a
plastic bag. He wasn't expected to live for long. She
plopped him in the dead terrapin's tank: watched him
loop. Blessed his tank: named him after her ex-fiancé,
the paratrooper: the one who'd chucked her out on the
street, howling. Godfrey.

Godfrey was like Godfrey: he was quick, ginger,
flash, but he was never mean.

He was so *bright* in our dingy house. He blew air
kisses all day, puffed out silvery smoke rings ... link
chains. A stray sunbeam hit his glossy water and he
sparkled. Round and round: an endless U-ey ... At
first, Majella blew him kisses back, showered him with
presents from the pet shop: bright coral-gravels, a
pagoda, a stone-coloured hide'n'seek boot, a fluor-
escent pink plastic hanging garden ... and sieved him
out, with the tea-strainer, for long transatlantic journeys in the bath – and then she *turned*. She turned to

....

clubbing, drugging, and a bloke called either Mr Ecstasy or Marv. Or both. Majella, my sister, went *rave* mad.

One day Majella was a laughter-line in a nightie, spitting on an iron, singeing a pleat down her navy work skirt, and next, she was this gum-snapping *stranger* pacing up our hall: wearing tight T-shirts with daisies on them, calling cabs at midnight; hipped out, with her belly button sticking out of flab. (Later, she had it pierced: it went septic. Septicaemia . . . She got gangrene. She had to go to hospital. It went the size of a yeasty currant bun. But that was *much* later.)

Majella really *loved* Godfrey but, after she hit the clubbing scene, got, as she called it, 'loved up', she hated him.

Listening outside her door I heard her chant above her telly, 'Ignore me now army boy. You *bastard*. You *bastard* Godfrey. What are you? You *bastard* Godfrey . . .'

I didn't think pretty Godfrey could live for long.

I was studying for A levels at the time, training hard as a Young Novelist, honing my powers of observation in little red note pads. (When I got my grades, the predicted A, A, A, I'd get to university five hundred miles away: leave home without one look back. I had to stay focused, unattached.) But I couldn't resist saving Godfrey. One wriggle in his tank, and I was hooked!

'Mum?' I said. '*Look*!' I'd airlifted him out from the hellhole of Majella's bedroom: blown away his sky of talcum powder, reeled out a foot of Majella's tan-coloured, scummy tights, and set him down by the scummy cooker in the kitchen. Though he was thin – a red bone in a white sock – he was, I thought, *all the light in our house boiled down*.

. . . .

65

In the hot kitchen Godfrey blinked his gold. 'Look Mum,' I said, 'Isn't he *sweeeet*?'

Mum looked down: her cheeks steamed, flushed like two rubbed spots. Her eyes, under her sweaty eyebrows, gleamed. I looked from her, to the brown sudsy cooking pots, back to Godfrey, back to Mum.

I thought: Poor Godfrey, he won't last for long. Out of the fire, into the pan.

Mum had gone ... funny in the head. That's what Majella yelled, tapping her temple: 'You're *funny-in-the-head*,' as though Mum's head had been stacked (when we weren't looking) with comic books, sitcoms ... I couldn't think of a better explanation myself. As I noted, in my novel-training note pads, when Mum *went funny* she went like Majella: *like that!* One day the air was a soft brown wall of unflushed loos, rusting geraniums, takeaway foods. Dust snuffed from the carpets thick as bonemeal. All day Mum made secret-recipe soups: threw great slop waves across the lawns. She'd scour the cupboards for odd ingredients. In went Majella's old school tie, an aubergine, one cake of cherry shoe polish ... Out puffed rust and rubble, scents that made the plants cave in.

Outside, our other pets howled on the lawns, sang like exiles, made a heady high white noise, scribbled their nibbled light-pink legs in the sheds, kicked up for dinner time. The toy poodles shook their pale dreadlocks. Our albino rabbits stretched their dirty jaws. Across the neighbourhood, strays joined in: cats caterwauled. Mum stirred away in the kitchen. She boomed a silent radar: her animal attraction. The pets on the lawns crackled, eared up and somersaulted back. Or they'd bounce and pose above the grassy gore, suspended for a moment, hunched like fridge magnets.

In his tank Godfrey (plumped up), beaming bright,

....

would pause. He'd leap above the pagoda, hang out in the hanging garden. Dirty strobe light smacked his back. His tail thumped. He swam on.

We had to ring for takeaways. At night, when the cat songs got too much, I'd lob our leftover cartons of chicken tikka, the chewy rinds from our takeaway pizzas, salty chip rejects, up out and into the long splattered grass. Shrieks! A scrummage. A feral pet race. The air filled with clods of earth: back-kicked peas. Tree-high stalks shook. As I noted in my red note pads, only the very fast survived.

Doctor Trang upped Mum's medication. The side effects, he said (zombie-ism, intense communion with small dumb animals), were a small price to pay, believe him. I did. I'd already noted the symptoms: synchronicity: in the hot kitchen, when Mum paused, holding a ladle, Godfrey paused too; when one stirred, the other whizzed rapidly round.

In the kitchen Godfrey's light drew me to him. He surfed the surface; flayed gold .. green .. red. His tank bubbled like a miniature Jacuzzi: full of air and spinning fat globes. He'd flip on his side, fin a zippy sidestroke, blow a little link kiss at Mum as she sipped, with deep concentration, at her wooden spoon. Mum looked down at Godfrey and blew him a crumb, a grape, a rubber fish face. They were one.

At least, I knew, with Mum around, Godfrey was safe.

At night, dust snowed around me. My plimsolls squeaked on the sticky lino. Never mind, I told myself, opening my revision notes, I'll be up in Loughborough soon . . . maybe Edinburgh. Wales. The University of Ulster? Miles and miles away . . . Somewhere clean. I vowed then, catching glitter scales from Godfrey, a tinkle tune from deep down in the blue pagoda, when,

....

eventually, I escaped, Godfrey was coming with me too. 'Godfrey,' I urged, '*stay* strong.' 'Manchester,' I whispered. 'Newcastle. Durham . . . You, Godfrey, and me.'

At night, our other pets sat in line on the black grass: ruby-red-eyed. They were the lifers: all born to us, given to us, at a time when we must have seemed, no, we were *exactly* like a photograph happily framed: there was Mum in rose-tinted C&A blouse; Dad, roastily tanned in his crisp blue cotton overalls. Majella and me in our steam-ironed bottle-green school uniforms (Majella's big hands on my little shoulders), showing our heavy-metal orthodontistry. Behind us surged a thunderous studio sky. Around us hopped the albino rabbits, the tortoise. The mongrels. The cats. Poodles . . . They all began to die.

Majella started clubbing it once a week, then twice . . . thrice . . . Mr Marv was a light voice on the line (a 'Yeah', a 'She in?'). He was a slice of shadow, a stripe of Adidas in the crack of a cab. Majella came home shiny, she sniffed, snapped her chewing gum at Godfrey. (Her luminous inks flowered first in the choke of the hall.) In the kitchen she drank tap water, spat green tubes of it through gaps in her teeth at me, at my homework; stared in at Godfrey as he flashed to and fro in his tank. Her face greyed, grew stone. She hovered over his tank, dribbled strands of her long beige hair in, eyes set wide apart: black-pooled, scary, like a shark's. Godfrey cowered in his hide'n'seek boot. I cowered too. 'Godfrey,' Majella chanted, 'I'm going to *get* you. What am I going to do Godfrey? *Get* you.' I didn't think Godfrey could survive for long.

Mum filled up pots, slopped the rejects out in long brown rattling arcs. Soup skin wobbled on the grass,

. . . .

shone like satin wheels. Pets raced from the sheds, squacked.

In the kitchen her pots heaved. A carrot went in. A bicycle pump, a jagged tin . . . Mum had the radio tuned to LBC. Godfrey swam rapids in his tank. His jowls flopped. His movements grew fevered. His tail rudder really whipped froth along. His little face, pressing flat for a moment against the glass, began to look quite – sad. Perhaps it was Majella? Ceaseless LBC? A tiny slit in Mum's synchronicity? Flitting across his features I'd see the face-mask of an ex-pet: one of the terrapins: Sandy? Andy? . . . One of those who'd dried.

Outside on the lawns, all the pets cried.

In my trainee note pads, I noted, sipping a Lemsip, 'We're all on medication now.' Mum had little white pills. Majella had her little white pills. Even Dad, who I was in love with, took massive painkillers. He had migraine. He'd come home from the railways like a train. Light stabbed him. Coffee killed him. Pineapple juice made him cry. He had migraine so bad he had to inject himself in the bathroom, using his leather belt as a tourniquet. (His injection kit was a toy briefcase, deadly black; inside, chrome cylinders, needles so thick they made your skin lock.) He had blinders. He'd charge home honking noise, smoking rust, with one eye spinning like a shot blue marble, the other scrunching up his forehead, his bobble hat thick with dust. I don't think he noticed the litter under his boots, or chicken tikka again for tea. I stood in the kitchen sipping black-currant Lemsip, studying my books, peeping in at Godfrey as he swam round . . . round.

Godfrey swam. He swam in brackish oily water and then, it seemed, he was deep in soup. He paddled past florets of cauliflower, dived under broccoli bombs, breasted logs of carrots, stinking shreds of chicken and

. . . .

lamb. He moved not in water but in stuff he really had to fin through. Gazpacho. The air flowed with stock. Godfrey gave little shivery, fastidious leaps. Mum, stirring, leaped too. Leaning, trying to talk sense into Mum, one day, yelling above the radio blah-blah of LBC, I saw Godfrey take a leap at the edge. But the walls of the terrapin tank were too high. He leapt but a stray *calamaro* ringed his neck, winched it back, cut his arrow-like route to the floor. My heart flipped. Godfrey's battered, swollen, mottled, white-veined mouth glugged each time, sank to blank – down amongst the greasy olives, baggy purple prunes, hairy anchovies swishing by like unshaved legs: the assorted mucus beneath the murk. I'd mumble above his surface: 'Leeds ... Aberystwyth ... Godfrey, you hang on.' I changed Godfrey's water but Mum souped it straight back up. I tried putting Godfrey in my bedroom near my computer and neat stacks of homework but Mum kept bringing him down, sloshing, bashing his delicate lips brown. I tried to keep Godfrey on the up.

But I failed. I failed my mocks. An (un-predicted) D, D, E. When I told Godfrey he flickered away. I looked for him in the grey TV screen of his tank. 'I'm sorry, Godfrey,' I said. I turned to Mum. She stirred away.

I tried to stay focused, stay head-down, but ...

I thought Majella was now heavily into the drug scene, was like a suburban drug queen, and I was worried. In the high streets, on Saturdays, she walked like a celebrity, in dark glasses, like *Ms* Ecstasy, grinding from the hip. Cruddy people tried to talk to her. Hordes of dirty, whey-faced kids whispered around her, begging for crumbs, for 'disco biscuits'. Majella brushed them off and, with a swing of her shiny nylon ginger hair-piece, a flick of her reddening belly button, she

....

mooched away. She had loads of money. Notes fell around her, folded up, tiny.

I saw adverts in the papers for people to appear and confess personal family information on *Esther* or on *Vanessa* and I was thinking of appearing. I'd snitch Majella up for her own good. I'd get her into rehab. Write to her from my tidy room. I circled the adverts with red biro and left them on Majella's littered grey bed, as a warning, a hint for her to *pull herself together*. I tapped Mum's arm in the kitchen. 'Mum?' Godfrey paused. 'Godfrey?' I said. 'Newcastle Polytechnic? Brighton FE?' Godfrey swam away.

Majella started clubbing it four times a week, five. She'd come home at around four o'clock in the morning, with Mr Marv. (She'd sleep maybe two hours, then speed off to work. Her eyes were like slots.) I'd wait up, reassuring Godfrey they'd be no game-playing tonight whatsoever, watching as his sides bulged at the scrape of a key . . . Mr Marv swung in first: smirked, picked up a dirty fork, toyed with its crusty prong, slid it up his sleeve. Majella doubled behind him: they were thin, shiny, daisy-topped. They'd sloppy-kiss, edge to the tank; rub each other up, but I was on guard, stayed solid, watched for the sudden lunge, the stabbing fork. They'd kiss out. Then, without warning, double back, *crash* into the kitchen tooled up to play, in between licks and despite my protestations, the Get Godfrey Game. They forked but Godfrey dived under the blue pagoda. They stabbed but Godfrey ducked into the hide'n'seek boot. He whizzed rapidly around a roast spud. Watching his dive I *felt* the full surge of his life force: he'd leapt back from a death wish; got firmly back *into* the swim; he swam away. Majella and Marv forked up sodden Cocoa-Pops, fried clumps of wire

. . . .

wool, crumbless stiff blue fingers of fish. Godfrey lived to flicker away.

Godfrey survived all through Majella's Marv stage, her Darren & speed stage, her LSD-plus-E stage. His stroke became really butch, determined. His nose grew blunt from speeding U-ies against the glass. Majella went clubbing six times a week. She looked thin-skinned. I could see the blood network through her face. She'd come home haggard in her Nat West uniform looking forty years old and emerge from her room, hours later, remarkably refreshed; showing tight arse-cleavage, her cheeks sparkly like two just-peeled spuds, her hair with a wide road of centre-parting, looking *just* eleven years old. In a rare burst of sister-hood, once, she showed me the three moves I'd need should I ever give up being a 'snitchy-bitch' and take up clubbing instead:
1 You put your fingers in the air and stab as though you're telling someone to piss off a lot.
2 You dance like snakes would.
3 You maintain an ironic hipster pose at all times.
But the music didn't really make sense to me: it seemed to consist of just the *one* sustained note and then random others! I couldn't see the point in all the drug-taking. I preferred, as a student Novelist, the occasional Lemsip, a paracetamol for my increasingly tense and nervous headaches, and life in the raw.

Our other pets went funny, *funnier*, in the head: showed acute symptoms of distress, neuroses, when they heard the squeal of a taxi. They bounced up and down on the grass, paced two steps forward, two steps back.
    At night, sitting up with my computer, I'd hear Majella come home with a club drone, a Clive, a Tyrone, a Jeff . . . and I'd wait for the screaming to

. . . .

start. A yapping; barking. Squeaking. Flash of a pen-knife. Then, the rabbits would start. Carnage. Lights snapping on and off in the neighbourhood: the grass electrified . . . shapes darting in and out of the sheds. One night I saw Mr Marv, Clive and Majella wipe blood from their mouths, a bit of white fur, a ridged bone, streaking through the grass, and I fell back on my bed and thought: I've got to leave this family *now*. I had to keep racing down to protect Godfrey from the Get Godfrey Games. In the kitchen Majella stabbed at his tank, screamed out her old howling rage, stabbed, as though Godfrey really was her *ex*-Godfrey, the keen-eyed paratrooper; as though she really expected a thick hairy wrist, a fist of fat freckled fingers, to spring from the tank: *Attack*! Godfrey ducked and dived, slithered and writhed: survived. On bad nights Mum had to run down in her nightie to quieten the dawn chorus squacking up the pear trees, squalling from the sheds. She'd raise her long arms and shush the insects lying crippled and crying on the broken but still-swinging greasy black grass. The cats and dogs, the rabbits and shield-less peeled tortoi staggered up the bloody garden paths to have their wounds licked.

Summer was awful. I failed my A levels and then I failed my resits (Fs). Tiny died in the sheds (she was all loose inside, really awful, like a bag of curds), and then Twinkle got run over. The tortoi fell into a coma and died. Suzi developed some kind of tumour on her neck and started going for Dad as he stepped in through the door from work. Really for *his* neck. Like *flying* through the air, like hiding under the stairs or crouched in the airing cupboard like Patience on a stack of dank sheets . . . The vet said a tumour removal operation would cost about forty pounds. One day I came in from signing on and Suzi wasn't there. Dad

. . . .

said she'd gone: 'Doggone'. He'd probably let her loose on the motorway, the bastard.

So we only had Godfrey left.

And Godfrey was getting bigger.

He lived on juicy blue flies that fell from the ceiling and cod in butter sauce. He really liked chips. If you plopped a chip in the tank Godfrey gobbled it down in one, like a piranha. Godfrey was so fat now he could barely turn around in his tank. He swam on though. He only paused in his heavy front crawl to listen to Mum's long radio monologues or watch her manic hands chop the air. He still blew her kiss and kiss kiss. Mum gleamed. She poured old cups of sugary sun-warmed tea on his back to keep his water level up, pulled a few rubbery fish faces; flipped in chips. With each look-in Godfrey swam with extra verve; blew out kiss and . . . kiss and . . . kiss. Sometimes, Mum kissed back. As the kitchen boiled up, Godfrey's tank became just like another steaming bowl of soup: he smelt, some-times, really tasty.

I wasn't so happy then. I tried to keep my spirits up by writing an epic novel slowly by computer in the morning and swimming slowly in the swimming pool down the road in the afternoon. I was quite good at breaststroke and, as I breasted the clear blue water, I thought about Godfrey: his immense powers of endur-ance, his selflessness. I admired the sheer *purity* of his direction. His staying power. I would, I told myself, now eschew all Lemsips and paracetamol. I would be as Godfrey, and simply *endure*.

Dad started coming home late, becalmed, with rust marks like vicious love bites on his neck. I noted his clothes no longer billowed their usual bluey-grey cloud of concrete dust. Had he shaken it elsewhere? I thought: Yes. (I imagined a bottle-blonde in a nylon

....

cream cardigan donned like a cloak . . . I drew a picture
of her in my notebook, stabbed big juicy blackheads
into her chin.) His boots also had new bootlaces on
them. I swam and listed clues like that. I was even
more worried about Majella. I could *smell* her rotting
flesh. It smelt light green. I'd be up guarding Godfrey,
watching late-night Hindu films on the telly, waiting for
dawn to crack light across the old chicken tikka cartons
on the still black lawns: I'd wait for Majella to come
home. Majella staggered from her cab. I'd smell her
first: rot. She'd come up daisies in the hall, push straight
through me, sneer, throw the drug literature I'd got
from Dr Trang back in my face, push me off. Her
forehead and temples were glossed with sweat; above
her hipsters the belly button rose from its punctured
hood like a lump of red, still-cooking, bread. 'Majella?'
I called. I had Dettol on hand, TCP ready. Majella staggered past me, zigzagged up the stairs, shook the light
fittings, and slammed a heavy screen of dust from her
door frame.

Godfrey swam in his tank. Gulped, slowly, round.

Mum's medications went haywire. She was talking
more or less out loud: answering all the voices chanting
inside her head. Under Dr Trang's direction she had to
swallow his pills and lift her flabby grey tongue for his
inspection. Mum swallowed. The muscles in her throat
rippled. Dr Trang shook his head, perplexed, and
wrinkled his nose.

Mum talked back to LBC on the radio, nodded vigor-
ously at whichever other airwave was tuning her in . . .
fuzzing her out. A new pet-fan squeaked from the
bread bin: a pet mouse. The mouse begged at her heels
as she stirred the soup. Or it climbed onto the beige
stubble plains of her worn-out carpet slippers, shiny
pink mouse marigolds signing up supplications; squeak
plaintive. Mum stirred the soup. The mouse scampered

. . . .

75

up her leg, her sleeve, her muscled arm, onto her shoulder, turned somersaults, squivelled, squeaked for attention, its cute black persistent eyes gleaming. Mum stirred on. The mouse cut a squeak through her airways. Godfrey, in his tank, splished up distraction: whacked up prawns, corn on the cob . . . splashed. The mouse tricked on. Wandering into the kitchen one hot after-noon, chewing my hand, I heard a – different squeak. Human: 'A carrot *is* essential, mango chut – . . .' The mouse was poised up on Mum's thumb, paws in beg mode, raised so its whiskers could tickle her own. Mum was squeaking, in a squeaky Nice-Aunty voice, the secret of her secret-recipe soups. She roared: *'Vanilla essence obviously, stupid mouse, ha, ha, ha, fluff! One cornflake, leather thong . . .'*

Godfrey broke surface. Red-eyed. Slowly dived. He no longer got a look-in.

Mum petted the mouse. She bound it to her gold wedding band, confided sauce notes at its peaked and quivery carpet-felt ears; WHEEED it through a peak-trough-PEAK roller coaster ride of brown kitchen soup air: all day. Or, with no warning she leapt decibels: SHRIEKED! Godfrey swam on ignored, like me, up and down. Up and slowly, solidly, down.

By day, stinking of chlorine, I wrote out job applications and listed my Reasons for Application. Sometimes I sat in my old dark-green school uniform adding a new chapter to my opus: Chapter 67 . . . Chapter 110. Or I'd look through my thumbed, smudged A level text books and wonder how and exactly *at which point* I failed. At night I stared into Godfrey's tank and synchronised with his one thought: Swim *on*. Just *swim* on. *Swim* swim swim.

Then one day I came home from a dole recall inter-view, chewing my lip. I thought I'd just look in on

. . . .

old Godfrey and start a really pure and positive Zen afternoon: Go on. Just *get* on. Chapter 200. Chapter 201 . . . I caught Mum leaning over Godfrey's tank. She was sly-faced, hugely pored. Her mouse-fan was boxing with excitement, shrieking squeaks from the bowl of her collar bone; it leapt at her stiff ponytailed head, climbed her ponytail scaffold. Wheeeeed round. The mouse grinned as Mum, gum frilled, tippled and dribbled the contents out of her brown pill bag.

The little white pills slid on a slide through Godfrey's murk, became, I noted, with their powdery star tails, like ultra-white planets in flux. I saw Godfrey buoyed up by half a cheese'n'viscous roll, by a boiled egg, pickled and embryonic like new baby skin – pause. The Planets glazed his right side-eye, shock-waved, rearranged. You . . . *good* Godfrey, I urged, Ignore. Just swim *on* . . . Godfrey. You *swim* on! Godfrey swam on, swam and swam on till, with a flash of tail rudder, a shiver, a final soup-thwacking U-ey, he – gulped. His throat rippled and he gulped again.

I went into the garden and, lying out among the stale pizza crusts, with big raindrops splashing on my forehead, I began to cry.

Godfrey lay at the bottom of the tank, slowly burbling, like a miniature ginger whale.

Doctor Trang gave me pills. I had growing pains he said. He patted my hand kindly and suggested I wash more. I smelt a bit fishy. I was a pretty little thing underneath all those eyebrows. I wandered the high streets, up and down, as the drugs made me march, and thought about a new novel I would write by hand, using pencil. No more computers. I'd get back into the raw.

In the kitchen, Mum shouted at the mouse-fan and the mouse-fan ran to fetch a friend. The two mice looked up and nervously conferred as Mum ranted and

....

confused them, sent a pea-green football flying off her wooden spoon. They chased.

I bent my knees to the tank and looked, with my slow-motion blink rate, into the thunderous grey matter where something large and orange glowed. 'I forgive you, Godfrey,' I said, reaching for a fork. 'I'm . . .' I stabbed, stammering, 'o-out of it ta-*too*.' I smelt light green: saw, on my periphery, luminous daisies bloom. 'Godfrey,' I said, 'the ga-game is o-*o-ver*.' Godfrey bellied up. Beside me, I heard Majella sob.

I Went Too Far

....

BRENT HODGSON

I bought those magazines: you know the type I am talking about. I collected a heap of them. Finally, I was convinced by what I saw and what I read in those magazines. I went to see a friend. She understood.

Take three a day, she advised me.

I took three a day to begin with. But I grew impatient: I took more than three.

Soon I was on twelve a day. I passed through the skin-and-bone phase; that did not bother me. I knew I was in a bad way when I started to fall apart: then I felt I had gone too far.

I made an appointment to see my dokta. His name is Flowerpot. I cannot tell you why he has that name; perhaps he wore a flowerpot on his head when he was a student of medicine?

My God, said Dokta Flowerpot when I entered his surgery; I was expecting Joe Swiggins to be my next patient.

I am Joe Swiggins, I said.

Joe! You have a problem?

Yes, it is like this, Dokta Flowerpot: I am losing too many slimming tablets. They seem to go straight through me.

Hop up on the couch, Joe, while I have a proper look at you.

He got out his auriscope to examine my organ of hearing. He could not find either ear.

....

This looks bad Joe, he told me in confidence.

I lay on the couch, too frightened to move.

Take a deep breath, Joe, my dokta requested, I want to check the tidal volume of air going into and out of your lungs.

What should the tidal volume be? I asked.

Five hundred millilitres.

I breathed in and out.

Dokta Flowerpot was unable to determine the volume.

Try deep breathing, he urged me.

I breathed deeply, forcing the extraordinary muscles of respiration into play.

Yet I sensed something was dreadfully wrong.

Where are the muscles surrounding your thoracic cage? the dokta questioned me.

Why, are they not there?

I can see your clavicle and sternum, twelve pairs of ribs – as you would expect – but the muscles holding together the bony framework of your thoracic cage seem to be missing.

That is all very well, I said, getting a wee bit angry; but what is wrong with me?

Joe, you said you have been taking slimming tablets . . .

Only three a day, I lied.

I think you have gone too far; the tablets keep falling through you because you have become a skeleton.

The minute he said that, I knew what was wrong with me!

I can stop taking the tablets then? I asked.

I cannot see why you would wish to take any more; you have lost a lot of weight, have you not?

I have; in fact, my weight is the lowest it has ever been! Oh Dokta Flowerpot, this is good news. Those slimming tablets cost a small fortune to buy.

. . . .

Now do not go running away, Joe, warned Dokta Flowerpot; you need a prescription for a reel of twenty-three-gauge copper wire.

Whatever for?

To hold yourself together, man; look at my surgery floor – and he pointed to the soft brown carpet.

There on the carpet lay four of my phalanges – toe bones, I later discovered – and one patella, a bone associated with the knee joint.

Nosferatu, the Valley Gyrl

MARINA BLAKE

I'm totally premenstrual. I thought once I became a vampire I'd stop having periods, but hey – it's one of the pitfalls the horror writers don't tell you about. Anne Rice doesn't mention it. Bram Stoker certainly doesn't. I haven't come across any writers who've referred to menstruating vampires. And believe me, I'm an expert.

The worst thing about bleeding is that it makes me so fucking hungry. Then I feel guilty because I think I'm killing more than I need. Yesterday, I went to a health food shop to ask the herbal specialist for help. He recommended Evening Primrose Oil, EPO to frequent users.

'Are there any side effects?' I asked him.

'None that have been documented,' he said.

He seemed like a nice guy. A little too skinny for a kill, and besides, I might need his help again if I ever have to go through menopause.

'I eat quite a lot of . . .' I paused, thinking about the best way to phrase it. 'I have a very carnivorous diet. Will that affect the EPO?'

'No, there shouldn't be any problem.'

So I started taking the stuff. I haven't noticed any difference yet, but it's only been one day. What do I want – a miracle?

That makes me wonder – if a miracle is the impossible

made possible by an act of God, can vampires be granted miracles? I'd love to stop having periods. Maybe I should start praying.

Meanwhile, I'm here in a café, having some tea, my abdomen cramping and my breasts swollen and painful to the touch. There's a screaming brat at the next table giving me a headache. *A mid-evening snack*. She won't be screaming much longer if I can get her away from her fat, overbearing mother.

One of the reasons I like young kills is that I've been very concerned about AIDS recently. Infants are in a low-risk category. Them and older people. But I don't like old blood. If the coffin-dodger is still in pretty good shape, it's OK. Not my favorite meal, but edible. But the old ones who never exercise taste rotten. Literally – rotten. Believe it or not, the other day as I was sucking on this old guy's neck, I could taste the decay in his body. It was totally gross. People should have a little consideration.

But the AIDS thing really bothers me. One of the advantages of being a nocturnal bloodsucker is that I'm not susceptible to colds or the flu, but AIDS still freaks me out. And you could say that, due to my intimate contact with other people's bodily fluids, I am in a high-risk group. But hey, the water'll kill you. The air'll kill you. And now the food'll kill you. We all have to die sometime. Actually, *you* have to die sometime. I don't . . . unless I get AIDS. Man, I have to get off this subject. It's really bumming me out. Really puts me off my dinner.

Talking about dinner, I'll have to go shopping soon. I like to hit the nightclubs. I pick up a guy, tell him I want to fuck him but can't take him home because I have a boyfriend. He usually suggests his place, but when I act horny and anxious, he settles for a fuck in

....

the toilets. I prefer it that way because there's very little mess. I don't even have to worry about the body. And afterwards, I can get a bit of clubbing in – maybe smoke a little grass to mellow out – before I call it a night and go home.

I'm not feeling very mellow at the moment. It's that screaming brat. And I don't need any grass. I need to suck the life out of her. She'll only grow up to be a junkie or a fat housewife like her mother. I'd probably be doing them both a favor. Later on tonight, after dinner, I'm going to the movies. Maybe I'll pick up a guy so I don't have to go on my own, but afterwards I'd probably want to kill him. So maybe I won't bother.

The movie I'm going to watch is *Nosferatu, the Vampyre*. I always go to the late-night showing of it whenever it's on. Klaus Kinski's great as Count Dracula, but I always feel a little sad after watching the film because it makes me homesick. Kinski reminds me of my dad, who I don't get to see very often since I left LA. Sometimes I phone him, but the time difference and our crazy schedules mean I usually get his answering machine. I'm a poor letter writer, and he only reads archaic Transylvanian anyway – which I can't write – so I don't see the point in sending letters. Sometimes I send him packages, though. A few years ago, I sent him a beautiful red cape. But he told me he wouldn't wear it because red is one of the LA gang colors. He usually doesn't get hassled by anyone because he looks like he's dead anyway, but he's old-fashioned and likes to play it safe.

One myth I'd like to dispel right now is that vampires sleep in coffins. Who'd want to sleep in a death box? That would be creepy. Vampires haven't slept in them for thousands of years. A vampire sleeping in a coffin would be like people still living in caves.

....

I live in a beautiful house on the outskirts of London. I had the basement converted into a huge bedroom. There aren't any windows of course, but I hung floor-to-ceiling black velvet drapes to cover up the gray brick walls. Most of the furniture is red velvet, silk and satin. I have expensive taste but I can afford it, so why not treat myself?

I don't ever bring the kills home because their smell gets into everything. Once I brought a young boy home – I felt like a takeaway instead of eating out – but, just like bad Indian food, his smell lingered for days. I even had to get the drapes cleaned. Another rule I have is never to go for female kills unless they're very young (like my mid-evening snack over there) because the hormones in their blood throw my system off. I'm neur-otic enough when I'm premenstrual; I don't need any more freak-out hormones on top of my own.

I discovered this important guideline when I once went for a menopausal woman. I wouldn't have killed her because I wasn't hungry, but she pissed me off. I was sitting in a café at my favorite table by the window, peacefully reading the paper and drinking my coffee. This woman came in and asked me if I minded her sitting at my table. I said no, as long as she didn't smoke. She said she'd smoke if she wanted to. I told her to find another table. She said no, she was going to sit at mine and she was going to smoke. This pissed me off because there were empty tables she could sit at. But I didn't want to call attention to myself. So I quietly told her to shove her cigarettes up her cunt. Then I took my coffee and my newspaper to an empty table. After about ten minutes, she came over to me.

'Do you know what you did to me?' she asked.

'Fuck off,' I said.

'Do you know what you did? You just verbally raped

....

me. Like a man would rape a woman, you just did that to me.'

'Fuck off.'

'Where are you from?' she asked.

I looked up at her. 'Fuck off.'

'Are you American? Is that where you're from? America? Is that how people act in your country? That would explain it.' Then she turned and walked out of the café.

I wasn't insulted, but I feel we all have a duty to discourage xenophobia. So I followed her home and did the business. I didn't know she was in the middle of menopause. I soon found out. I cried every day for three weeks. I haven't gone for a post-pubescent female since then.

This screaming kid brings me back to the present. My head is pounding from her shrill whingeing. I finish my tea, go to the toilet and leave. I have an hour before the movie starts. Since I haven't eaten yet, I go in search of food. As I walk by a back alley, I see a drunk, twenty-something man peeing against the wall. *Perfect*.

After dinner, I head for the cinema. The kill's drunkenness starts to hit me, and I feel slightly wobbly. I realize how stupid my choice of kill was. I'm premenstrual. He was drunk. I'm now premenstrual and drunk. *Will I ever learn?*

I'm walking along the street, next to a graveyard, and as I turn the corner I see a young couple ahead of me. They're walking arm in arm and their laughter echoes across the street and back. The woman throws her head back and laughs again. They stop and kiss. I pass by them quickly, not wanting to be seen or heard. When I get to the cinema I stand in line to buy my ticket. Suddenly, the tears are coming. I have no control over them.

....

I run to the toilets and shut myself in one of the stalls. I'm so lonely. How did I get to be so lonely? I have no friends, no lover, no children. The only pet I ever had was a friendly cat that became the appetizer in a night of gorging when I felt uncontrollably violent. I have a beautiful house and live in as much comfort as I want. But I have no one to kiss goodnight, no one to laugh with or meet in a café and drink green tea with.

I suddenly get an idea. I pull the bottle of EPO out of my purse and swallow all the capsules dry. It's a bottle of sixty. At least I'll find out if the stuff works. After a little while I feel calmer. I blow my nose and wipe my eyes. Pulling the tissue away from my face I notice the tears are pink. Must be dehydrated. I'm not so sure it's a good idea to watch the movie in my present emotional state, but since I'm here I might as well stay. At the ticket counter, handing over the money, the ticket guy's hand brushes mine.

He looks at me, then away. He blushes. He looks like he's in his early twenties.

'Thanks,' I say as he hands me the ticket.

'You come here every time we show *Nosferatu*, don't you?'

'Yes.' I think he's going to say something but he doesn't. 'Would you like to go for a drink when it gets out?' I ask. He's probably not interested, but I just want to be near someone.

He looks nervous. 'OK,' he said. Then he smiles, and I feel a million years old.

'OK. See you after the film.'

I go find a seat, picking up a Coke on the way. There are a few previews – nothing I'm interested in. The opening sequence of *Nosferatu, the Vampyre* comes up. Skulls. Wasted, shrunken, dried-out bodies. Rows and rows of them. I start to feel a little better. The familiarity

....

of the film reminds me that I've been here before and that how I feel now will pass. My loneliness will be replaced by something else – probably hunger. There is a cycle, and I'm part of it. It's only natural to feel down sometimes.

But then, toward the end, everyone's dying and there's nothing left but rats. Rats everywhere. Nosferatu can't find love, and neither can I. All we'll ever be left with is rats.

I close my eyes. I'm so tired. So tired.

I decide to stay up and watch the sunrise. It's been a long time since I've seen the sun. I run out of the theater before I can change my mind. The ticket boy is so beautiful, and if I don't run away from him fast, I'll make him ugly. Ugly and dead. I run until I'm out of the city.

When I get to the coast, I walk along the shore for a while. Then I sit on a large rock at the edge of the water. I remember a Chinese man who lived a few houses down the road from me when I was a little girl. He showed me how to chant different Buddhist mantras. I followed his instruction for many years. Then when I became a vampire, he was my first kill. I chant Om, the seed sound of the universe. Om. Om. The sound of creation and the sound of destruction. I close my eyes and chant. The next time I look up, the first rays of sunlight are skimming over the water towards me.

Moving Target

GORDON LEGGE

Rancey's old dear phoned him at his work one day, telling him as how he was to go over to his Auntie Teen's, round in Clouston Street, and pick up a wardrobe for his sister Janice that was moving into her own place over the old town.

Rancey said, 'Aye, no problem,' and once everybody was off home for the night, he popped out his hidey-hole, pocketed Mat's spare keys, and helped himself to a wee shot of the works van.

Now, wardrobes were normally two-man jobs, but Rancey never bothered himself with hunting round for volunteers. Nah, it would be a challenge tackling this on his own: and Rancey fair liked his challenges, especially those that called for a combination of Rancey's brain and Rancey's brawn – mind and muscle jobs, as he called them.

It had been years since Rancey had last been at his Auntie Teen's, and as he cracked open a can and headed round – with the windows wide open and the stereo blaring out Queen's Greatest Hits Vol. 2 – Rancey tried to see what he could mind of the old place.

And the first thing that came to mind was his old dear's warning – 'Now, don't you dare touch a thing. You hear me?' Reason being that Auntie Teen's was forever decked out with all these fragile-looking wee

....

89

ornaments the two boys, Auntie Teen's sons, brought back from all their travels with the navy.

Rancey had a wee laugh to himself. For all that he'd never once actually got round to meeting up with the two boys, Rancey was never shy when it came to mentioning them – as in, 'Mess with me and you mess with my cousins – and they're in the navy!'

But the navy didn't sound hard enough, it wasn't hard enough for Rancey, so Rancey changed it first to the army, then the marines, and eventually it became that his two cousins he'd never once met did top-secret assignments for the SAS. That did the trick. If anybody was hassling him, Rancey would just grab a hold of them by the throat and go, 'Mess with me and you mess with my cousins – and they're in the SAS!'

The funny thing with all this, of course, was that the boys out the navy weren't really Rancey's cousins, and Auntie Teen wasn't really Rancey's auntie. Rancey was just to call them that when he was wee. Not that Rancey was complaining. Big families meant hard families, and Rancey adopted any relatives he could. He even invented them: his Uncle Alec that was in the jail, his Uncle Grant that had the gun, his Uncle Davie that . . .

Rancey's brain stopped in its tracks.

Clouston Street! Flaming Clouston Street!

His Auntie Teen was staying upstairs in a four-in-a-block in Clouston Street – and the scum that was Whitey and Bammo stayed upstairs in a four-in-a-block in Clouston Street and all.

No, it couldn't be, could it?

But as Rancey pulled into Clouston Street, the two sad facts became just the one sad fact – his poor old Auntie Teen, all on her lonesome and coming to the end of her days, was having to live through the wall from the bog-washed, festering vermin that passed for Whitey and Bammo.

....

Rancey parked his van. He'd hold on a minute before heading up. Rancey was needing to think about this.

Whitey and Bammo were druggies – and as far as Rancey was concerned the sooner all druggies met their maker the better. Talk about a waste of space. All the sorry scum ever thought to do with itself was to sit in its poxy wee house with its poxy wee pals, listening to its poxy wee music, watching its poxy wee videos, and spending its entire poxy wee life smashed out its pin-sized poxy wee skull.

For all that, mind, all that poxy stuff, the thing that really bugged Rancey about druggies, the thing that totally done his head in, was that arrogance, that arrogant look druggies always had on them, that *I know something you don't know*; like they were all supposed to be so smart or something, going on like wee lassies in the playground. That's all they were and all, wee lassies, daft wee lassies. 'I know something you don't know/ And I'm not gonni tell you/ Na-na na-na nah nah.'

Rancey had only ever been in at Whitey and Bammo's the five times. It would always be the same – one of his mates would be wanting a bit blow, and what with every other source in the town run dry, they'd've ended up at Whitey and Bammo's; where, ritually, you got teased by the kids, got attacked by the cats and you had to listen to Frank fucking Zappa. 'Zappaaaaahhhh!' as Whitey called him. 'Zappaaaaahhhh!'

The last time he'd been round there, Rancey'd looked through the pile of records, dug out the first Motorhead LP, bunged it on, turned up the volume, and pogoed away to his heart's content. Should've seen their faces. Rancey thought it was a scream.

And so did all his mates when Rancey told them. Rancey was forever telling stories about Whitey and

....

Bammo. The classic was the one when Bammo's old boy had went round to have it out with them. Bammo's old boy was none too happy with Bammo for having teamed up with the slothful Whitey, and had went through their bedroom, pulled the covers off their bed and dropped the big brown one all over their mattress. Fucking classic.

Despite the fact Rancey told this as gospel and everybody duly passed it on as such, the origin of the story lay that bit closer to home – for in truth it was Rancey's ex who'd shat on Rancey's mattress.

But Rancey wasn't one for wasting a good story, so he gave it the most deserving home he could think of. Anyway, Whitey and Bammo just set themselves up to be laughed at – and Rancey hated folk like that. Rods, he called them, just total Rods.

Apparently, Whitey'd been in Rancey's year at the school, but Rancey could hardly mind of him. Just one of those wimps Rancey and his mates used to waste when Rancey and his mates used to spend their playtimes going round wasting wimps. Bammo, on the other hand, was one Rancey did mind. Rancey had quite fancied Bammo at the school. Mean, she was nothing special, but she was all right, she was worth a poke. When Rancey had grabbed a hold of her one day and told her that, though, told her how she was worth a poke, Bammo'd went all funny. Not that Rancey was bothered; he'd got a decent feel of her tits before she ran away.

These days, Rancey wouldn't've went near Bammo even if she'd been gagging for it. Bammo had went right ugly. Lost it completely. The last time Rancey'd seen her, she'd had her head shaved up the sides and what meat there was would've struggled to feed a veggie.

No, Rancey couldn't get angry with the likes of

....

Whitey and Bammo, and as he went round the back of his van, for his rope, his four cushions, his broom handle and his slippy bit wood, Rancey couldn't help but notice just how run down and decrepit the old street was looking.

And there was no doubting in Rancey's mind as to who was responsible – Whitey and Bammo.

Rancey went up the path. He chapped his Auntie Teen's door. He tried the handle but the door was locked.

The old bint was probably getting a bit deaf in her old age so Rancey knelt down and shouted through the letter-box.

'AUNTIETEEN!... IT'S... ME... RAN-... CEY... COME... FOR... WAR – '

'Henry?'

'Ih?' Rancey turned round. It was this wee wifie in T-shirt and jeans with Bammo.

'Auntie Teen?'

'My, Henry, it's a fair old while since I last clapped eyes on you. Stand up, and let me have a look at you.'

Rancey stood up.

'Goodness, what a fine figure of a man you've turned out to be. Bet you don't remember the last time you seen me, do you?'

Rancey shrugged.

'It was Portobello, the summer of '76. Mind, you came through with me and your Uncle Tom? That was the day you shat yourself and wouldn't admit to it.'

'I never did!'

'You did so,' said Auntie Teen, 'and don't you go denying it. What a state you were in, laddie, the slitters all running down your bare wee legs.'

Bammo was laughing. Rancey scowled at her. Bammo still had her head shaved up the sides. What hair there was was yellow and all done up like string.

....

She had rings through her left nostril and her right eyebrow. A fucking mess, in other words.

'I'll see you later then, Romy,' said Bammo. 'Thanks for your help.' She went away.

'*Romy?*' said Rancey.

'My new name,' said Auntie Teen. 'You not like it, Henry?'

'No, I don't. I think I'll just stick with Auntie Teen, Auntie Teen.'

'Suit yourself. Come on then, let's see about getting this brute shifted.'

They went up the stairs.

'What was spaghetti-heid wanting?'

'Sorry?'

'The pin cushion, whatsherface.' Rancey tried to mind Bammo's Sunday name.

'Bammo?'

'Aye, her.'

'Oh, nothing, just having a rake through the greenhouse, seeing if there was anything she could make use of.'

I'll bet, thought Rancey. Anything she could sell, more like. Right, that settled it. Auntie Teen was needing straightened out about a few things.

'Any chance of a cuppa before getting started?'

'Oh, I'm sure we can manage that.'

There was this right funny smell bugging Rancey as they went up the stairs. The only thing Rancey could think to compare it with would be sticking his nose into an old, empty crisp packet.

When they reached the kitchen the smell grew worse and Rancey's jaw just about dropped like an anchor. Talk about a bomb site. Every cupboard was open and all the worktops and tables were all covered with these spice jars and packets of stuff. Rancey picked one up and had a sniff.

....

'Hey, Auntie Teen, this's off. No best be putting it in the bucket.'

Auntie Teen sniffed at it. 'No, it's all right, Henry. It's supposed to be like that. Now, what sort of tea can we do you for?'

Rancey shrugged.

'Let's see, we've got . . .'

Auntie Teen listed half a dozen types of tea.

'I'll just have whatever you're having, Auntie Teen.'

Auntie Teen stuck the kettle on. Rancey started putting away the spice jars and stuff.

'No, Henry, don't bother, just leave them. I won't be able to find anything if you put them away.'

'But, Auntie Teen, they make the place untidy.'

Not for the first time, Auntie Teen shrugged.

This was doing Rancey's head in. Rancey'd always been brought up to believe that if there existed one wee bit of dirt or one wee bit of untidiness then there was always somebody, somewhere that seen it – and that was why you kept everything clean and tidy. And if you didn't keep everything clean and tidy then you got whacked on the back of the legs with the poker, got sent to your room and got told not to come down till it snowed blue snow.

'Now are you sure, Auntie Teen? Mean, it's no bother.'

'Oh, I'm sure all right. My generation's wasted too much of its time as it is with all this blasted clean and tidy carry-on. It's neither wonder we made such a right mess of things.'

The kettle clicked off and they went through the living room.

'Eh, Auntie Teen,' said Rancey, 'why've you got a rug nailed to your wall?'

'You not like it, Henry?'

Rancey shook his head. He didn't like the tree sitting

....

in the corner either. Or the fact that there wasn't a carpet. Or a telly. Or anywhere to sit.

All the chairs were upright chairs and you only ever sat at upright chairs when you were sitting down to your Christmas dinner.

'Auntie Teen,' said Rancey, 'where's your suite?'

Auntie Teen sipped her tea and pointed next door.

Rancey was beeling. 'They did what? You wanting me to go get it back?'

'Och no, Henry, don't be silly. They wanted a suite, I gave them mine. No harm done. That thing was far too big for in here.' Auntie Teen sat down. 'Anyway, these chairs are better for you. Good for the posture. Picked them up for a fiver at a silent auction. Not bad, eh?'

Rancey shook his head. He made a seat from his four cushions and sank into it. 'If you don't mind me asking, Auntie Teen, how much did your suite cost?'

'Twelve hundred I think it was. I never liked it, though. It was your bloody Uncle Tom that was into all that keeping up with the Joneses stuff. That daft clown was always buying up expensive rubbish that was neither use to man nor beast.'

Bloody Uncle Tom? That daft clown? You didn't speak of your dearly departed as being 'bloody Uncle Tom' or 'that daft clown'.

'You must miss Uncle Tom, though, eh?' said Rancey.

Auntie Teen shook her head. 'Best thing that ever happened to me. If I'd've murdered him I'd only've got half the sentence I did when I married him.'

'Auntie Teen!'

'What, Henry?'

'Uncle Tom was a nice man.'

'Oh, he was nice, there was nothing wrong with him; but he was a boring bastard, Henry, and that's no way

....

to go through life. Always the house: the house first, the house second, the house bloody everything.'

Rancey's ears twitched. There was music coming from somewhere. Rancey went over and put his ear up to the wall.

'Right, you wanting me to go and have a wee word with them, Auntie Teen. It's no problem.'

'Away,' said Auntie Teen. 'A wee bit music never hurt anybody. After all, it's only Za-ppaaaaahhhh!'

Auntie Teen giggled.

Rancey freaked.

'That's crap, Auntie Teen, that's absolute crap. There's nobody alive should have to put up with that. You know what that is? That's noise pollution. You can get folk put away for that. I'll just go and have a wee word and they'll never bother you again.'

'Away, away and behave yourself. Now, sit down, drink your tea and stop making such a fuss.'

Rancey did as he was told. He sipped his tea – it tasted like the wrapping you got a boiled sweet in. Bogging.

'To tell the truth,' said Auntie Teen, 'I think Zappa's shite and all. I'll put a wee bit of this on and we'll see what you make of it.'

Auntie Teen switched on this ghetto blaster that was down beside her and soon this really freaky music started coming out from over beside the tree and from over beside the door leading out to the lobby. Ambient shite, as Rancey called it.

In the meantime, Auntie Teen leaned back and stretched herself out like she'd been poleaxed. Then she started speaking really slowly, like one of them hypnotists. 'Now, just you try and relax yourself, Henry. Just take a good sip of your tea and just try and relax. Just concentrate on the tips of your toes, and just relax. Just concentrate on the tips of your fingers,

....

just relax. Just listen to the music. Just relax. Then all the way up, up through all your joints and up through all your veins, just slowly let yourself relax.'

Rancey took a sip of his tea, concentrated on his fingertips, listened to the music and tried to relax.

After a few seconds, though, he was starting to feel really weird, so he decided instead to think about battering fuck out of Whitey.

There you go. That was better. Rancey was due to give somebody a skelping, anyway, and Whitey was perfect: what with being a druggie, what with being a wimp and what with taking a loan of his Auntie Teen, Whitey was singing for it.

'How you doing, Henry?'

'Oh, feeling good, Auntie Teen, feeling shit hot.'

All Rancey had to do was to find something that pissed off his Auntie Teen when it came to Whitey and Bammo.

'So,' he said, 'that pair next door, been getting any bother off them?'

Rancey was watching her. She was thinking.

'No, not that I can think of.'

'What about the noise and that, I've heard that the likes of them can give off some racket.'

She was thinking again. 'There was one time . . .'

'Aye,' said Rancey. That would do. One time would do.

'Yes, now that I come to think of it there was the one time; but apparently that wasn't them, just some clown that was round visiting, put on this really loud music – Motorhead, I think they said it was – and started jumping about all over the place. Bammo said that the poor fellow wasn't all there, mind you, so I suppose we should excuse him.'

Wasn't all there? Wasn't all fucking there?

Whitey had just signed his death warrant.

....

Whitey was getting wasted. Whitey was getting himself seriously wasted. The hi-fi, it was getting wasted and all. The hi-fi was getting mega-wasted. 'Just out of interest,' said Rancey, 'where's your telly, Auntie Teen?'

'Oh, I bunged that monstrosity next door and all.'

Rancey shook his head. She was away. She was away with the goddamn fairies.

'Henry, don't laugh, dear. But doesn't it bother you that you know more people on television than you know in real life?'

Rancey thought about it. 'So?'

'Well,' said Auntie Teen, 'I don't know about you, Henry, but I find that alarming. Mean, how are folk supposed to get on when all they ever see of each other is on that stupid bloody box?'

'Hold on,' said Rancey. 'Auntie Teen, are you feeling all right? I mean, in yourself, are you all right?'

Auntie Teen got up out her chair, grabbed a hold of her right ankle then wrapped it round her neck. 'Feeling fine, Henry,' she said, 'feeling fine.'

This was getting too much. Now Rancey's brain always worked best once he'd worked up a bit sweat, so he drank up the last of his tea and said, 'Right, come on then, let's have a look at this wardrobe.'

They went through the room; and there was the wardrobe. It was a fucker. It was the sort of wardrobe you'd expect to find holding Betty's going-out gear at Buckingham Palace.

'Are you wanting me to give Whitey a shout?'

Rancey sneered. He gave the wardrobe a budge. It was about the weight of a small car. Rancey shifted one side eighteen inches then he went round and shifted the other side eighteen inches.

The plan was to edge it to the top of the stairs – and once it was at the top of the stairs, well, it was easy enough to get to the bottom of the stairs.

....

'Auntie Teen,' said Rancey, 'I don't want to alarm you or anything but what you've got staying through the wall there are a pair of good-for-nothing druggies.'

Auntie Teen laughed. 'Come on, Henry,' she said, 'lighten up, will you, it's only hash.'

'What?'

'I said, it's only hash.'

'Auntie Teen, listen, I know about these things – it's a chemical, it gets in their brains, it messes them up, it makes them paranoid, it makes them scruffy.'

'It's all to do with how you use it, Henry. It's just like anything else: you mustn't be a slave. There's no such thing as freedom unless you exercise your freedom. That's what I keep telling them.'

Aye, aye. Rancey thought he could be onto something here. He shifted the wardrobe another eighteen inches. 'So you have a go at them then, eh?'

'Well, I wouldn't put it like that, but I certainly speak my mind. See, Henry, I've had all this before with your Uncle Tom: his drug was buying things, buying up useless rubbish. You know he held me back. He never thought to exercise his freedom, so I never got any.' Rancey was half concentrating on this, half concentrating on the wardrobe.

'So, that pair next door, you think they're as bad as Uncle Tom.' Rancey was minding as how she'd said she'd wished she'd murdered Uncle Tom.

'In a way, yes.'

Good, problem solved then. Rancey would just go round and say, 'See you, Auntie Teen says you're as bad as Uncle Tom.' Then he'd start wasting. You know, it really was amazing how things became that much clearer once you worked up a bit sweat.

'Aye,' said Rancey, 'druggies: no consideration; wrapped up in their own wee worlds; smashed out their

....

skulls morning, noon and night. Best just to keep out their road.'

'I do think they go a bit far,' said Auntie Teen. 'Personally speaking, I only ever tan a spliff if I want to get myself zonked out.'

And at that moment, in lieu of this wee bit of unexpected information, the wardrobe didn't so much land on Rancey's foot as appear to wilfully crush Rancey's foot.

'Goodness, Henry, are you all right?'

Rancey stared at her. He wasn't going to scream. No way was he going to scream.

'Henry, d'you want me to get an ambulance?'

Rancey shook his head. He somehow managed to get a hold of the wardrobe and get it shifted.

The foot was throbbing like something out a cartoon. Rancey bent down and counted his toes. There were still five, but one seemed to be awfy detached from the others – it was like trying to catch a goldfish, whenever he touched it, it went away, it was like it wasn't . . .

'Henry,' said Auntie Teen, 'Henry, you've gone a funny colour.'

He'd severed a toe. He'd severed a fucking toe.

Of all the things to do, Rancey started smiling. He stood up. He looked like a statue of Rancey. He'd severed a toe, he was in absolute agony, and he hadn't screamed or even shed a tear. This was how hard he was.

Rancey could feel the toe moving about. He didn't want to cause it any damage so he took off his trainer and shifted the toe so's it came to rest under the arch of his foot.

That way, if he walked with a banana foot he'd be all right.

Rancey got back to shifting the wardrobe. Whitey was getting it; for being a druggie, for being a wimp

. . . .

and for turning Auntie Teen into a twenty-four carat flakehead, Whitey was going to get the most seriously severe kicking any living creature had ever got.

Rancey was hoping and praying there were going to be others there, other druggies – Rancey was wanting a mass-wasting, a mass-mega-wasting.

The wardrobe was now at the top of the stairs. The sweat was lashing off Rancey like he'd just stepped out a chip pan.

'Now, Henry, have you worked out how you're going to get it down?'

'Got a plan,' said Rancey. 'Got a ten-point plan.'

Rancey went through the living room and collected his rope, his four cushions, his broom handle and his slippy bit wood.

On his way back, however, something truly disgusting happened, and Rancey let loose the most piercing scream this side of an abattoir.

Auntie Teen rushed through. 'My God, Henry,' she said, 'are you all right?'

Rancey nodded. He'd forgotten to walk with a banana foot.

Hence, he was standing on his toe.

He was standing on his fucking toe.

'Just needing a drink of water,' said Rancey.

Rancey went through the kitchen. He slammed the door behind him.

He took off his trainer and sock. The severed toe looked like an uncooked oven chip covered in tomato sauce. His foot looked like something out a butcher's back yard.

Rancey opened up the freezer and scraped at the ice with a fish slice. He scooped the ice into the sock that contained the severed toe, and, once he had enough, tied a knot in the sock, and stuffed the toe-containing sock down his other sock. He put ice in his trainer as

....

well. It was agony to walk on but Rancey suspected that in these circumstances this was what you were supposed to do.

Rancey hobbled out the kitchen.

'D'you not think we should maybe just call it a day, Henry?'

Rancey shook his head. He picked up his rope, his four cushions, his broom handle, and his slippy bit wood. 'Got a plan,' he said. 'Got a ten-point plan.'

Rancey put his plan into action, his ten-point plan:

1) The wardrobe was tilted and the slippy bit wood slid underneath.

2) The rope was secured loosely round the wardrobe.

3) The cushions were placed between the rope and wardrobe, then the rope was tightened.

4) The remaining rope was harnessed round Rancey's legs, arms and shoulders.

5) The wardrobe was edged forward so's it was balancing on the top step.

6) Rancey, tug-of-war style, wedged his left heel against the kitchen door and his right heel against the bathroom door.

7) Rancey picked up the broom handle. He put it in his mouth. Gently, he leaned forward till the broom handle made contact with the wardrobe.

8) The wardrobe went flying down the stairs.

9) Rancey took the strain.

10) The wardrobe came to rest on the bottom step.

Rancey looked at Auntie Teen. Auntie Teen looked at Rancey.

'It fucking worked,' said Rancey.

Auntie Teen nodded. 'Henry, forgive me for asking, but is that how they normally do it?'

Rancey shrugged. He'd dislocated a shoulder, he'd scorched his hands and the rope had cut right into his

....

family allowance . . . but, hey, come on, it had fucking worked. Rancey collected his broom handle and hobbled down the stairs.

It was perfect. There was no damage to the wardrobe, no damage to the wallpaper and he'd left just enough room so's to get the door open. Fucking brilliant. Rancey got his rope, his four cushions, his slippy bit wood and his broom handle, and hobbled the distance out to the van. It was seventeen hobbles from the door to the hedge, and five hobbles from the hedge to the van.

Rancey lay two of his cushions on the floor of the van, and placed the other two upright behind the driver's seat and the passenger's seat.

On his way back, Rancey saw Whitey and Bammo at their kitchen window. Even from this far away, and through the net curtain, Rancey could still make out that look, that arrogant look, that druggies look – that look that Rancey was going to wipe right off their faces for once and for all. Rancey gave them the finger. *I know something you don't know. I'm gonni kill you!*

Rancey got the wardrobe out onto the path no problem, then gave it a quarter-turn so's it was broadside on. Subtlety bit the dust – Rancey was tackling this turtle-style.

It would have to go up to get over the hedge, then down to get into the van. Rancey repeated this to himself a couple of times so's he wouldn't get mixed up.

Rancey tilted the wardrobe. It weighed a ton and it wasn't even off the deck.

He took deep breaths. When he reached ten he'd go. One . . . two . . . three . . . four . . .

But Rancey couldn't be bothered hanging about. He went on the five.

Seventeen hobbles to the gate . . . sixteen . . . fifteen . . . fourteen . . .

. . . .

When Rancey reached hobble number two he shouted, 'Geronimo!' and straightened his arms.

The pain was beyond pain. Every part of Rancey that could snap, snapped; every part that could burst, burst; every part that could tear, tore. Rancey managed four more hobbles then flung himself forward.

The wardrobe landed in the back of the van.

Rancey smacked his head off the bumper.

He gave himself a count of eight before getting to his feet. He was okay.

More importantly, so was the wardrobe. Perfect landing.

Not a scratch, not a fucking scratch.

Auntie Teen came down the path.

'I did it,' said Rancey. 'I fucking did it.'

'That you did, Henry, that you certainly did.'

That was the worst of it, anyway. Rancey could just dump the wardrobe at his sister's and let them get on with it. Then he'd head straight up casualty, get his toe stitched back on, get his shoulder reset, get his head, back and hands looked at then return and batter fuck out of Whitey.

'Well, it's been nice seeing you, Henry,' said Auntie Teen. 'Hope you don't leave it so long till your next visit.'

Rancey nodded. Aye, right. He wasn't bothered whether he ever saw the old flake again or not. He got into his van, opened a can, downed it in a oner, then turned the stereo on – 'I Want To Break Free' – then sneered at his Auntie Teen in his side-view mirror and headed off.

Halfway down Clouston Street, however, a small ginger cat came bombing out onto the road.

Rancey swerved to avoid it.

Then he thought to himself – why the fuck was he swerving to avoid a stupid bloody cat?

....

It was too late.

The van went off the road and smacked right into a lamppost. Rancey went clean through the windscreen. His good shoulder shoulder-charged the lamppost.

The last thing Rancey was thinking before his head hit the pavement was how he hoped there wasn't a scratch on the wardrobe – cause if there was a scratch on the wardrobe then his mum and his sister Janice would surely kill him.

Back outside the four-in-a-block Auntie Teen had been joined by Whitey, Bammo – and a small ginger cat.

'And you're sure,' said Bammo, 'he doesn't have insurance?'

Auntie Teen shook her head. 'No dear: no insurance, no license, he's on probation, the van's been reported stolen, and going by his breath he's over the limit. Poor Henry's going from hospital to jail.'

Whitey and Bammo held each other's hand.

'Well,' said Auntie Teen, 'I suppose somebody better go and dial 999. See you later, instigators.'

Auntie Teen headed off.

'Romy,' said Bammo, 'there's still one thing I don't understand.'

'Yes, dear; and what's that?'

'Well, we've good enough reason to hate him, but – why you, why d'you hate him?'

Auntie Teen laughed. 'D'you know, Bammo, I couldn't really tell you; but it's a funny thing, these days I really do get a kick out of knowing things that other folk don't.'

And with that Auntie Teen winked at Whitey and Bammo and went upstairs – whistling to herself as she did so a daft wee tune, a daft wee tune she hadn't whistled since schooldays.

....

'No Exit' Always Means an Exit

ELIZABETH YOUNG

'Easy to control but... a junkie whore is a boring creature to have around.'

Mad Dog McKenna interviewed by Gerard John Shaefer, Florida State Prison Death House, Starke, FLA 32091 USA.

'There would never be enough time to count that much money. We weigh it. Twenty pounds of hundred-dollar bills is about a million dollars. So, a hundred pounds of twenty-dollar bills is the same. A million. Sort them that way. A hundred million, five hundred million – *no es problema.*'

You are waiting for the man. The man is a woman called Carrie. Slipping and a-sliding down the long hill in the autumn sleet. And that's the way the money goes. Slipping away round the back in the night like Carrie herself. Nothing is still long enough to really see it. Always changing but always the same. If you stare out the window hard enough and long enough you think you can see her, coming round the corner, trying to guide the pram over iced and broken tarmac. Fifteen storeys up, fifteen storeys and what do you get, another day older and deeper in debt and you can definitely see her, she shines out like a star among the dark cloud of homebound commuters, she's the source of all hopefulness, source of all joy, she's the doorbell that rings, setting off sudden fireworks of ecstasy in your head, the nearest you will ever get to pure pleasure – of any kind – and now she's in the lift, she's left the pram downstairs, the ice on her ponytail has started to melt, she's steadying her bulk against the fractious grips and jerks of an ancient system; the wires are going. Her bare knees are stinging with the blue and purple tattoos of the English winter wind. One sticky bandage uncoils towards her plimsoll exposing a black trench in Carrie's calf; 'big enough to hide Napoleon's army in' he had said last summer and they had all laughed and laughed and it's bigger now and she's mouthing like a hooked fish in the peephole and she thrusts the bundle at you. It's so heavy, hot, sweet and damp beneath the crochet whorls and roused by the shove the baby opens its mouth and loses the dummy. White, utilitarian as a plug, it rolls floorwards. 'Poor sweet, poor sweetheart,' you murmur, you can be generous stretching out these precious, silvery filaments of anticipation. Warmth and easy love, this is as happy as you will ever be ... You've forgotten its name. Atishoo? Carrie hoists her skirt. 'Letisha'. Apricot silk cami-knickers with the tiny explosions of blood across their sheen, making rust of dingy lace trim and beneath them bikini bottoms and beneath them and beneath them the dust of grey fur, the rat's bite of the trapdoor and the glutinous pink and white and plastic. This woman eats her own blood. In clots, from a saucer in case she misses a trace. Letisha, Letisha, we all fall down. We all ... you knew this coke dealer, up in Stoke New-ington, they called their first child, a daughter, Charlie, to keep the good luck running their way. But – your mind has got to wandering and you see there's no one

....

108

on the hill and no one even bowling outwards in the hot dust from the Tube entrance any more. Each streetlight shows the nothing and the great night rushes back into you all at once; as hideous as memory, as twistingly painful as hope. If you go down and go out and try and phone Carrie from the box she'll flash past while you're over the road. Sod's Law – it's always like that, she only rings the bell once, she barely waits. Why should she? It's cold out there. And there are so many of you. What shall you do, what shall you ever do . . .?

And Mad Dog McKenna said 'Put a girl on rock and she'll do whatever you want to get more.' What happens to them all?

They go together like a horse and carriage. H and C. Horse and Carriage. Hot and Cold, H and C. Uptown, downtown, night and day. There is a sigh at the heart of the world, the empty seesaw quivers, the chain-link fences sing, the lightning slices across a deserted playground in hell. There lay the original sin, the ruination of unity, the splitting of the one into two and thenceforth onwards for ever, condemning us not just to life – the old fear and torture routine for ever – but to half-life. Born hooked at the wrist to a corpse, a skeleton, a blank. We must animate or assimilate this dead other that accompanies us through all the long minutes of living as the playthings of dualism. Merge, blend, join, find peace.

How many times have people on opiates said – plaintive, stubborn – 'It makes me feel whole'? How many have been unable to endure this withdrawal of apparent unity and the enforced return to the endless restlessness, daily crawling of nerves, and constant bolts of panic that signify ordinary life?

. . . .

How the people point and stare. They don't want to hear more about the eschatology of escapism, the aesthetics of indulgence, the ease of gratification or the legislative horrors of prohibition. They have seen the quick scribble of quasi-fashionable accessories too often. The spoon, the flame, the spike, the mirror; the impedimenta of incompetence. If they know it they need to forget it. If they don't it is as unimaginable as non-existence. They don't want more claims and counterclaims, topplingly erected upon so many generations of misinformation and deception that the entire edifice now stands timeless miles from where it should. To take this situation-comedy seriously is to court derision, to hijack a Pickford's van and move right into that town without pity.

But tonight all over the planet they'll be creeping out again, from the dachas, from pastel-coloured duplexes in the temperate zone, into a couple of pick-up trucks. Like raggedy-andy Halloween revellers they take the white cotton sheets and the sharpened stakes – oh and the radios and guns and flashlights – and they drive out to the flat place, the pasture, the lonely place where the boulders and mesquite trees have been cleared. The trucks are stationed at each end of the strip. The men hear the throb of the solitary, incomer twin-prop plane and they hit the headlights, spread the bed sheets and run between them, hammering the stakes, each with a white paper plate nailed to it, into the ground. Aerocommanders, Aztecs, Cessnas 210, 206. Plan nine from outer space is grounded, the runway's clearly marked, the plane lurches down, they unload the bales that originated in the coca, the poppy, the hemp. Ten minutes and the plane lumbers towards takeoff, another five and all the trucks, all the equipment, all is gone. The bush, the jungle, the woods, the hills left

....

again to the shrieks of wildlife. Later we will all bathe
in the torrent of money that roars down on us, from
the mouth of the devil. Every night. All over the world.

In the Caymans and Bahamas, in Liechtenstein and
the Scillies the banks are jumping and jingling – bulging
with bogus corporations, front companies – trying to
hold more than the entire GNP of many countries.

'Look' says Jay, pushing the powder around, 'drug razor
art. Watch . . .' He slides the Mexican brown across
the mirror – 'What's this, gringo, hey?' Even the cat,
intrigued, rubs his throat against the edge of the coffee
table and purrs. Jay's blade forms a sombrero, two lines
for eyes, a line for nose and then the long, drooping
curves of a moustache are reflected back, deep into
the mirror. Everyone laughs. The cat jumps round, his
plumed tail switches quickly over the glass and sweeps
all the powder to the floor. Never mind. There is always
more. If you have the money. Someone blows a long,
bitter stream of narcotic smoke into the cat's little bud
nose.

Thera is waiting for the man. She has been a customer
for many years. She has never met this person. Nor
does she expect to. He's well organised. She rings a
mobile phone number. Someone, not always the same
person, answers and Thera ('It's Thera', first names
only) orders a one-hour – or three-and-a-half-hour, or
whatever – backing tape of house or hip-hop, classical
music or rock music. 'He's on his way now,' they always
say and Thera watching television or on the phone has
her ears preternaturally attuned to every street noise.
She is waiting for the unmistakable note of a bike dying
down and stopping and then the click of her garden
gate. She opens her front door to the pollen and diesel
clouds of a Kensington summer evening. Her orange

. . . .

roses, rimmed with rot, are a blur as she signs for the package, any name, Mary Thunder, this is as happy as she will ever be. If she doesn't like the powder, or the smack, or the rock, she can return it after her first try and it will be replaced. But they never pick up as quick as they deliver and no one ever holds out that long. Soon there's not enough to return, however shitty it was. Oh, Thera, Thera.

All roads lead to home for the chemically incontinent. It is always the same story. 1840, 1850, 1860 – onwards and upwards. And it's *up* for the tired, black stevedore, sweating there on the Canal Street docks, not far from old Perdido Street, hired by the day, paid by the hour, with coke for endurance and the lifelong burden of projecting the fantastical alter shadow of vengeance by night – barrel-chested and vast, a black djinn of the Delta, whose great engorged member is silvered with semen and when the pencil breaks and all scrying ceases is just a teenage boy on a lonely road, crying before a clot of inbred thugs, be-sheeted like kids, fingering a rope, with the bitter scorch of bourbon in their brain-dead jibes. Just as it's *down* for the Union soldier whose agonised entrails are shed to dispossess the South of just such cheap labour, to transport it north and herd it in the stockyards and beat it in the canning plants, fertiliser for Chicago and let it die of ptomaine, and cold rain and a long heart-sickness. And the soldier boy limps home to Cow Town USA with the vials in his pocket if there is morphine left to spare and he gives it to his great-aunts and he gives it to his cousins and their hearts beneath the calico beat with warmth and new good cheer and the mending doesn't look so bad although the soft fruits still need canning. And they get it from their doctors and they go to church on Sundays – until the Harrison Act is passed

....

and their backs are broken. Their suffering is brutal, these old ladies in their parlours. The flower arrangements are all dying and the silver all needs polishing but they are knotted with arthritis and back in pain for ever. And it's *down* too for the Chinese immigrant, vilified on Mott Street, San Francisco, China Town. Their pipes are carved with dragons with the poison in their jaws but it's *up* for their white slave victims, yellow roses, Texas virgins all of course, who can't resist strange footprints in the snow and the trap is sprung, inscrutable. The bonny girls each in her individual bamboo cage – they're sold from out the back rooms far behind the stretched and naked bright red ducks, drying into leather with the Pacific breeze.

Such viciousness, degeneracy. Get rid of foreign scum or they'll take their trade to England. Over there, nineteenth century, it's *down* for the Fen-folk children, seven to a bed, a wooden cot, they're sucking on a rag soaked in laudanum but soon it's *up* for the Chelsea flappers, giggling in Limehouse as they buy off Mr Brilliant Chang, spilling their beads in the CrabTree Club while the Tiger Lady sings; that hoarse and smoky voice. Harrods sells gelatine sheets soaked in morphine and cocaine during the Great War. The advertisement reads: 'A useful present for friends at the front.'

It's *up* for Carmen Miranda, stuffing the packet in her wedgie mules and lacing the silk ribbons, scarlet, pink and aubergine, around her glowing legs and it's *up* for Barbara La Marr, her coke in a silver salver on the grand piano, a blizzard of white roses lying across the polished wood, and it's *down* for Wally Reid, rending his flesh with his teeth in the death-throes of withdrawal locked up to die neglected, by the richest movie studio in the world, and it's *up* and *down* for the Weimar Republic, for Djuna Barnes, Charles Henri

....

Ford – vada the Vandervogel with their riah zhooshed up and all their slap . . . vada the trooper in black fishnet stockings with the bona dish down the cabaret . . . clone zone death starts here.

Post-war Britain was drenched with a flood of dirty, bitter, brown ale. A few scattered mavericks – Anna Kavan, Aleister Crowley, Alex Trocchi – got their hard drugs legally from their doctors. But by 1968 when the pendulum was swinging back this tolerant legislation was banished in alarm. US-style prohibition forbade the prescribing of heroin and cocaine and those who needed, those who wanted, were thrown to disease, disaster, imprisonment, crime, penury and the pointless daily round of desperation.

I, Cassie, first took heroin in 1969. In the school holidays. Easter. We left the Tube at High Street Kensington and walked westwards for a few yards. It was spring, one of those days that is sunny and sparkling for a instant, followed by a dark squall of rain. I was wearing an ankle-length sheath of midnight blue velvet, trimmed with heavy silver lace and brocade. Underneath I wore pale blue tights, nothing else. I was cold. My shoes were silver leather pumps raised on stripped pine platforms. My jewellery was silver and tin and amethyst, it left dark rings when I took it off. Tiny faux pearls were threaded on an unravelled hairnet through my hair which was black and flat and hung to my waist. My companion's hair was the same. He wore mirrored sunglasses and an embroidered waistcoat over a white shirt and scarlet bell-bottom trousers. He had been adopted as an infant by a couple in Kingston upon Thames. When they picked him up his only luggage was a miniature pair of boxing gloves left with him when his parents blew away.

....

We turned right into Hornton Street. We went up some steps to a house and rang a bell. A girl opened the door and stood back, buttoning up a dirty paisley shirt. Her eyes were closed.

'Is Pluto here?' my friend asked.

'No. They took him away three ambulances ago.'

But she led us down to the basement flat. Later I pushed up my sleeve and bared my arm and turned my head away. I heard all my bracelets sliding together with a solemn click. A brief flash of pain as with an immunisation shot and then an intense prickly heat and then I had to throw up. It must have been morphine. I didn't try again for many years. Of all the folk tales associated with narcotics one is most certainly true: if you don't get away from it in your first year or so you will take it for two decades. For the first eighteenth months of use, even regular use, withdrawals are fairly mild – yawning and scratching and sneezing and farting and shitting a lot and feeling too hot and too cold and too restless and not able to sleep – but no worse really than bad gastric flu. It is bearable, even in custody. But after a couple of years when every cell in your body has been altered and bonded to the foreign substance, when all your natural endorphins are finished ... then, well ... may *someone*, may *God* have mercy on you. This difference makes for a lot of bad misunderstandings, horrible juju. This is why some people die from complete withdrawal. Their captors think it isn't anything much, *no worse than the flu*. But that, for their victim, was long ago.

In Turkey, in the frozen fields, when they lay down the cabbages, they place an ounce of heroin in the heart of the baby plant. As it swells and grows over the summer the leaves overlap and tighten, hiding the package. Then they are harvested, great green footballs

....

and put into container lorries and they travel overland, past all the borders. Cassie will die of a cabbage overdose.

Edgar Poe can scarcely breathe in the tiny cottage. August. The trapped, fly-buzzing heat of the eastern seaboard. Flushed with tubercular temperature, irritated and enthralled by the nervy listlessness of his child bride, his cousin, he soaks himself in opioides. He may be ill-advised but he is not illegal. What everyone so deplores is his excessive drinking. Alcohol is the very devil. Without it America would have no problems, right?

But you could cry for Kurt Cobain, damned by being born in the one century when he cannot have opiates for chronic pain, bedevilled by this cruelty, misled by those still young enough to believe in such a thing as 'selling out . . .' Eventually everyone has to sell what they have and for most it is not very much and there are few buyers. Did he really think his critics would be jeering in the mosh pit and setting fire to their apartments twenty years on?

It is always the same story. Gin, absinthe, laudanum, opium, morphine. Reefers and cocktails, then cocaine. Acid and amyl, dex and barbs, PCP, MDA, peyote, mescaline, cocaine and smack. Perrier, steroids, Prozac, crack and then smack.

When the great storm of 1987 screamed over the South East, many said it was summoned by the descendants of the coven that had kept Hitler off this island. They work deep in some wood, a little Bermuda Triangle not far from Brighton where ramblers and even the local vicar has vanished and where pet dogs twist and whine and shiver if you try to drag them by. Well,

....

another working brought the storm and later the money markets crashed and the future went in a different direction. It rose after midnight, tearing giant oaks up by the roots, and sent the city dustbins crashing into upturned cars and before the lines went down the junkies called each other and then they battled down the backstreets and over railway sidings. They knew all the police were busy, racing round the crisis. All the alarms were going off, from shops and cars and houses. The chemist shops were waiting, pools of forgotten peace. It is easy to lever the DDU cabinet off the wall, with hammers and jacks and screwdrivers, crash it to the floor, smash it apart, no one can hear, the winds rip by, tip everything into a rucksack, don't forget the works – right there, the little diabetic ones, grab a handful, run – and back home they'll be heroes. Smugglers and pirates, scrabbling on the carpet, among the cat hairs in front of innumerable gas fires, playing with the ampoules, fire on glass, a thousand thousand ampoules.When the end comes, when the power grids fail, when the warning goes, find a chemist. Then a bookshop – I mean a gun shop.

At Studio 54, its great icon the moon would descend and the man in the moon snort up the electric crystals from a spoon. Sure, they got it a bit wrong but then they were all whacked out of their skulls. Cocaine is the feminine, the moon in its third aspect, seductress and destroyer. Irresistible, the silver web of Isis, Artemis, Cybele, sphinx and vampire, the secret mouth of the world, the devourer of souls whose breath is the plague, who suckles her serpents. She is Kalma the corpse-eater, Lamasthu, Lilith, Ashtaroth, Exael, Kali. In the southern latitudes she is Odudua, goddess of the dead and you must sacrifice the gore of white, white chickens. Or she is Coatlicue wearing a dress made of

....

serpents with a girdle of dismembered digits and still-beating hearts. Her coat is the flayed skin of her son and she dances upon his entrails as the drums beat out their monotone. She always smells of smoke and oranges, she takes her toll in blood and crusted flesh, she is electricity and energy. But she wanes, the little o shrinks and crumbles, sucking with it your feelings, your dreams, the brightest of your language. Shut your mouth, stop your ears, press your eyelids till the red sparks fly. If you see new pictures then you might just be able to slide away.

She is dust.

Living is hardest when it is emptiest. From kilim to shining kilim, the room is perfect. The sugar skulls, the beeswax candles on their iron spikes, the wooden triptych altarpiece, the Haring original. Bottles stand open, petals drift lazily from a frosting of baby's breath. The afternoon has stopped. The sun does not move in the sky. What do we do? How can we live here? Do we walk back and forth, back and forth?

Stacey is waiting for the man just outside the hotel, opposite the Hyde Park railings, trying to look as if she should be there, as if she is staying at the hotel and just catching an early cab to the airport. The first pink wash of dawn shows through the trees. Fritillaries of dew glisten like snake scales in the grass. Her man is her pimp, well, no, her boyfriend. Billy is from Glasgow and she hasn't known him that long but he has a good, one-bedroom Housing Association flat in Camden, near Primrose Hill. A big white house with a tangled garden, a Victorian conversion. Most nights he drives her west, often here. She's been wobbling up and down Bayswater all night in damp suede stilettos, now pushed deep in her koala bear rucksack. She's wearing light

....

canvas flats. Her feet are frozen, she can hardly feel them. She pulls her leather coat tighter. Billy bought it for her in Camden Market, so he says. He's still married to Sheena from up north who has their kids in a council block on the Marylebone Road. He seems to spend a lot of time there – or somewhere, but. He stopped by three or four hours ago to pick up her money so he could go score. Stacey, Sheena, Stacey peers into the gloom, hands in pockets, praying that each car will be the dark blue, reconditioned Ford Escort but it never is. The road shines. She tries to avoid the back-wash from the early buses. Tired, tired. Her chest and head are burning hot, drops of sweat forming on her upper lip, and round her hairline. She's clucking now. She prays he's got the gear. Sometimes he brings her a fried egg sarnie from the all-nighter. In her head they are home, on the rug in front of the gas fire, curtains drawn tight, in the one room they use. Her legs and toes are unfreezing, mottling. The Sky Movie channel is turned low. They are surrounded by paper-bags from Bliss's the all-night chemist, and orange plastic needle covers and polystyrene carton tops. She will never, never go back to Northallerton. God, she hopes he hasn't been nicked. Oh . . . not *tonight*. Not *any* night. He is so careful. A car dips its headlights at her and slows into a familiar silhouette. She blazes with joy.

Like Mad Dog MacKenna says, a junkie whore is kinda boring. Stacey knows she has nothing much to say. Her thoughts are peeled down to a bland neurological base, registering only the most primitive spark and hiss of neurons. Need, fear, relief.

And Dave is waiting near the Stonebridge estate where the cabs won't go. Waiting for Tyrone, endlessly animated, never to be contradicted, that's disrespect, jerking his worn skateboard with one foot, all his clothes too big, his laces trailing on the pavement.

. . . .

Handing over the saliva-slimed clingfilm, the poisonous debased freebase, between a rock and a hard place. And Jo and Essie, on the Breton waterfront, ducking into an after-hours *boîte* that's playing Jim Morrison's 'Whiskey Bar' and the Velvets very loud, if you close the door, the night will last for ever and they ask in mime, '*Attendez, oui, certainement*,' and now they wait, uneasy, francs in the saucer, drawing on their Gitanes. And Lisa, outside the English bookshop in Tangiers, pretending to look at the window display, her heart hammering. And Markie, driving every day down to South Central LA, past the fortress liquor shops and boarded projects, he saw a guy strangled once, he keeps a gun under the dashboard, although he has no idea how to fire it. Another truism, a folk memory. You always have to wait. All round the world, thy children sing thy song – from East and West their voices sweetly blend, praising the um . . . in whom all things are strong, da, da . . . our guide, our healer and our friend . . .

The opium principle stains all pantheons as well. In its natural form it was Morpheus, the poppy, and Lethe, Ganga, the slow, brown river of oblivion. Give, sympathise, control. In its later incarnations, its modern distillations of morphina for La Vida Loca, and heroin, it has segued into that ancient, ironic elemental, the trickster. Coyote, Loki, Edshu the Yoruba hoaxer god and from there the Santeria decision, Elegua, capricious, unpredictable and like Papa Legba in Haiti, the guardian of the crossroads.

For this is how it goes. Everything he gives somehow turns into its opposite, so subtly, so slowly. You take the dope and first it makes you very beautiful, thin as a needle, translucent, haunted, your cheekbones in relief. A decade on the same girl is bloated with water retention, her back is humped, her hair thin, her legs

. . . .

puffed up. No one would want to look. At first it wakes you up, you are brighter, sharper and then the magic turns sleepy, duller than the ditchwater in the veins. At first you are never, ever ill, no flu, no colds, such stamina. Later you are always sick, always tired, always hurting. At first you can say and do anything. Later, there is nothing left. All the black humour, all the bright animation drains away in the worst theft of all, the theft of your language, your adjectives, your wit. All gone.

And these fragments are the pattern of my ruin. Aged beyond sense there should be no forgiveness for this slow-stepping corpse, this old, fat, rich whore from the North, living on half a lifetime after death, in supplication to disgusting gods. As the lady says, there are always two deaths. The one the world knows about and the earlier one.

Brujo, throw the coco nuts again. You gentlemen, you *all* work for *me*.

Toilet Love

STEWART HOME

Like a lot of girls studying art history at my college, Emma Compton-Day came from an upper-class background. Her father had bought her a house in Portobello Road, which she shared with two other students, Rachel and Lindsay. I don't know why Emma took a fancy to me, but she did. I liked Emma a lot, but I didn't want to be her lover, she was too controlling. Rich girls are often like that; they think they can buy your obedience if you didn't enjoy a similarly privileged upbringing.

I'd gone over to Emma's flat because she'd promised to henna my hair. Lindsay was there with her boyfriend Paul. Rachel had gone out. Emma announced she had bought some LSD. I'd never had it before and I felt a little silly swallowing the blotter she gave me, since it looked more like a piece of paper than a dangerous drug. We made jokes about getting high and Emma proceeded to dye my hair. She was being quite provocative about it. I was sitting on a stool and she rubbed her pendulous breasts against my back as she worked her rubber-gloved fingers through my hair. Once the vegetable dye had been evenly applied, Emma placed the foil on top and directed the hot air from a hair dryer over my scalp.

Although Emma had done disco biscuits before, none of us had any experience of good old-fashioned LSD. After Lindsay made a second pot of tea, we began to joke about the drug not working, since it was taking a long time to have any effect. Eventually, I went through to take a leak. I gazed at the orange and white checked curtains. On the white squares there were orange flowers, and as I looked at the petals I noticed they were spinning around. I stared in amazement as I pissed, and once I'd finished I stood with my cock hanging out of my flies, totally engrossed by this psychedelic display.

Lindsay came into the bathroom, eased past and sat on the loo. I must have been staring at the flowers when Lindsay dropped her knickers, since I didn't see them fall. Lindsay took a piece of bog roll and used it to wipe the tip of my cock. Then she dropped the tissue between her legs, so that it fell into the toilet bowl. I looked down as I heard the sound of Lindsay's piss tinkling into the flush pan. She had my erect cock in her hand. Lindsay's head moved forward and she took my manhood into her mouth. I felt a shudder of pleasure travel up my spine as her neatly cut bob slid forward. Lindsay still had most of the shaft in her hand, and she manipulated it so that the head of my cock rubbed against the roof of her mouth.

Lindsay slavered over my plonker for quite some time. Then she stood up, placed her hands on my shoulders and pushed me to my knees. I thought girls usually dried themselves with toilet tissue, but Lindsay made me clean her twat with my tongue. When I'd tongued Lindsay to her satisfaction, she pulled me to the floor and guided my cock into her cunt. I don't know how long we were fucking, but it seemed as if time was standing still. Sometimes, Lindsay had her tongue in my mouth, at others she bit my ears, shoulders and neck.

'Are you shagging my girlfriend?' Paul asked as he wandered into the bathroom.

....

'No!' I replied indignantly.

'That's okay then,' Paul said. He left after pulling the tinfoil from my scalp, ducking my head into the toilet bowl and flushing the loo several times.

I'd shot my load on the final flush. Next, I got up and stumbled around until I remembered to pull my trousers up. I wandered into the hallway, where I found my bicycle, which I took with me as I made my way onto the street. I cycled until the noise of dub reggae booming from the upstairs room of a pub attracted my attention. I got off my bike and padlocked it to some railings. As I approached the glass door, a vicious-looking psychopath advanced towards me. I knew the worst thing I could do was show the slightest sign of fear, so I kept moving forward, until eventually I walked into my own reflection.

Inside the venue, people kept asking me for a quarter or an eighth. I was innocently replying that I didn't have any dope, only to be told repeatedly that I stank of it. Only later did I realise that the fresh henna in my hair was the cause of these hassles. I ducked into the toilet to escape the pressures of being mistaken for a dope dealer. I couldn't find the urinals and three girls doing their make-up gave me the evil eye. I locked myself into a cubical, sat down on the toilet and began to shit what I took to be ducks eggs. A girl invaded my space by climbing over from the cubical next door, while another crawled under the bottom of the door. The two vixens took my shoes off my feet, took my pants and trousers from around my ankles, then removed my shirt. One of the dolly birds fingered my balls, while the others went through my pockets.

'He hasn't got any dope!' the chick examining my clothes exclaimed.

'He must have smoked his stash,' the amazon

....

fingering my balls replied, 'look at the dozy sod, he's totally out of it! Shall I blow him anyway?'

'Yeah,' her mate replied.

The drug-starved sex-kitten bent down and took my cock in her mouth. When I came, my sperm blew out the foxy chick's brains. None the less, she managed to get up and walk away, so no real harm was done by my smoking gun. A girl who was doing her make-up helped me to find my clothes, then assisted me as I struggled to get dressed. Later, she got me to sit on a sink and painted my face. I wandered out into the street and found my bicycle. I rode into the night hallucinating that I was a comet zooming through the cosmos. After a while it struck me that since all the planets and meteors travel in circular orbits, I could end my trip, which had become rather unpleasant, by returning to Emma's house.

Eventually, I found myself back in Portobello Road. I'd more or less come down from the acid. I just wanted a piss before I crawled into a warm bed. Rachel led me into the house. I went into the bathroom and as I stood staring at the curtains, I noticed that the petals of the flowers printed onto them were spinning around. Emma came into the bathroom and sat on the toilet. She took a piece of bog roll and used it to wipe the tip of my cock. Emma had put on a blonde wig which slipped badly as she leaned forward to slaver over my dick . . .

. . . .

Half-Baked Alaska

TONI DAVIDSON

FAX POSTCARD TO CURTIS SAD, NOVEMBER 1996

Just been on an amazing walk, Sad, took the air in and blew the cobwebs out.

It's made me realise that I haven't been out the city in years, holed up in those whitewashed, institutional walls, banging my head against the tiles, watching others bang theirs. You forget how vicious that circle can get, eh? Even a psychiatrist can cry in the dim privacy of his own torment . . . shit, there I go. Back to the couch-chewing world. You've heard it all before. And yet here I am, in fact here we both are. The shrink and the patient; the therapist and the therapee. What a beautiful place for the fucked up.

Wish you were here.

Here's the spiel, here's the rhyme and reason for all that follows. It's been kind of an ambition of mine to combine stimulants and therapy where some kind of psychoactive drug is used as part of the treatment of a patient. Of course drugs and therapy have the kind of history that no one would want to shout from a hilltop even in scenery as beautiful as this. As good as the idea is – and believe me I've sweated this one out for some time, churning that reputation versus risk debate around my head again and again until I've been that close to jacking the whole thing in and getting myself a nice leather chair and a handful of safely neurotic patients – I need to separate it from the sterile, locked-door, ECT image of professional drug administration. Back at the Institute we have schizos aplenty, some quelled into near zombie-like status, dribbling their dreams away, others propelled into quasi-euphoria, dancers lost to some distant music, as well as a whole range of detriments – people who for one reason or another have found their way into our consulting rooms – who have ingested enough pills to fill these mountains. As you know, the image of drugs and therapy is not a good one and I have been kind of waiting for the opportunity to sidestep the expectations people have and maybe take some time to retrace the steps to a more authentic, more startling form of therapy.

Location is everything in this little theory of mine. It's no good being holed up in some office and speak of transcending established protocols and dusty treatment models, I need to be in a place like this – huge trees, steep mountains and rapid white water – where backdrop could influence process and vice versa; where the line between patient and doctor becomes indistinguishable and less than important.

Cutting-edge stuff in the Delong Mountains, Alaska.

I got to the cabin about eight hours ago with my mysterious stranger, my pale, waxy friend – darling to his parents, X21 to the files but Languid to you and me. Languid? It kind of suits him. And his problem? Well, he's an eighteen-year-old mute born to a family steeped in family traditions, big on the financial markets, who make the Amish look positively liberal. You hear what I'm saying, Sad, this family's got everything. Money, connections and power but what they don't have is a son they can parade around at parties and say '*Here's the next in line . . . but he doesn't say much . . . he's everything we expected . . .*'

. . . .

127

I'd be lying if I said that I was their first port of call; people like Languid's parents don't hang their dirty washing on the line, know what I mean. They came to me in my box-like office after having tried both the Church and beatings by way of a cure and while pushing Languid into a chair, they uttered for them what must have been a cry for help.

'Make him normal.'

'Normal?' I asked provocatively.

'Like us.'

This was a conventional family seeking solace in the unconventional.

Still, the timing was good, because as you know not only do I have these pet theories roaming around my head but I have also managed to wangle a combined travel and research grant *to bridge the gap between institution and environment, to take psychotherapy and psychological research on the road with the intention that milieu should be as important as technique.*

Well, it was a good pitch and here we are, a halfway house between the insane and sane worlds, in a log cabin at the foot of the Delong Mountains. With the idea in place and location and patient identified, fellow psychohacks and old college friends, Stretch and Wait, have been in contact to say they'll be along at some point over the weekend to invigorate proceedings with their own unique synthesis of provocation and stimulants. The picture is, as they say, complete. Don't breathe a word to a soul.

Languid's parents had agreed with surprising ease, all papers signed to that effect and Languid was handed over to my tender care and my undoubted expertise. The parents of course just want to have a ball for a weekend, let their hair down and get horny in the pool

....

without their morose child staring at them and not saying a word.

As far as they – and more importantly their friends – were concerned, Languid was away at a salubrious camp for the sons and daughters of the very rich indulging in all kinds of aquatic and exotic sports with children of his age and peerage. In actual fact Languid is sitting about five, ten metres away across the other side of the main room of the cabin staring out the window looking at the view. He hasn't said a word, of course; the whole trip up in the car he sat like a rock with me bantering away, tuning and retuning the radio trying to pick up on some sounds that might lurch him into the here and now. Amateur stuff, I know – he's no coma victim waiting on some star from stage and screen to record him a tape and jerk him out of his reverie with some prime time glitz. I know he's not like that but hey, it gives me an excuse to listen to some nasty music. I don't suppose his parents have tried rap as an alternative therapy. *Put your motherfucking hands in the air* . . .

He's transfixed but only by the scenery as far as I can see and who wouldn't be? What a view, what a place this is, Sad. Being here is an extension of that homespun philosophy that travel broadens the mind, that the self is replaced by some greater need for survival and location is, as they say, everything. If a patient lives in a world of silence take him to where silence is supreme; if the patient does not speak take him to a place where there are no words; if the patient has retreated into a world where he thinks he is the only person then take him to a world where he *is* the only person.

I knew from that first, nervous meeting with him and his parents that I was going to like the kid, felt as though I was going to be able to give and take with

. . . .

him. And I know I'm doing him a favour for even if nothing occurs or works because of this experiment and that this pet theory of mine is simply suppressed narcosis inspired by some chemical overdose as a result of sucking on my beatnik mother's placenta . . . I know I've taken him away from his filthy rich parents concerned only with their lineage and their image. They told me before I left about some of the therapists they had taken him to.

He's been through the lot, Sad, every third-rate charlatan in the city has seen a fat fee for trying to, as they see it, bring him out of his shell. Shit, the dollar signs must have been ringing in those fucks' eyes when this fur-coat brigade walked in. *Visualise this, regress to this, think about the first time you did that.* He's been through it all has Languid. If he wasn't fucked up before he went to these renegades of the rational then he surely is now. An office full of hypnotherapy junkies waiting in line for their newest failing to be exorcised or covered up, a thin layer of gravel over their drive, man; a couple of handfuls of soil over the shit they have just laid for themselves in their lives.

This fax machine is a soapbox, Sad, in case you hadn't noticed. If you look closely you can see the bubbles.

It wasn't that Languid's parents believed in all this shit, far from it; they were from the school of thought, that venerable and esteemed school that says: smack some sense into the little runt; whack the neuro out of him and make him a real man. Shit, the father wanted to send him to a military school in the hope that the drums and drills, the fake camaraderie would instil some normality in him. Stupid idea of course. The mother wanted to keep him at home and get tutors, doctors, anybody with a half-assed certificate to mend his silent ways. Not much better, and in the end nothing had worked and the last guy they had been to had broken the straw on the camel's back. Or whatever it is.

I know the guy as well, Sad; he tried to get a job in the Institute because he thought he was so shit-hot. He was on the crest of the recovered memory wave, surfing that fucking paddling pool of ideas. You remember? I'm talking about a few years back when the RM bandwagon was beginning to roll and this guy, Dr Raymond Churr, had written two books in the space of six months explaining the need for this kind of therapy and how analysis would never be the same. *Stop me if you've heard this one before* . . . He credited himself with 'discovering' many different types of memory: body memory, imagistic memory and – get this – feeling memory where he managed, having accumulated a host of pulped facts, to diagnose 100 per cent of sexual abuse in all his patients. These suckered patients, who no doubt fitted Burr's strict clinical criteria, i.e. that they should have more money than sense, were encouraged to describe a 'gut' feeling, a deep, bone-twisting, stomach-squeezing whopper of a memory that someone had touched their dick or cunt when they were a kid. This is the memory of emotional response Churr went on and on about. So of course when confronted with Languid, a boy of fifteen years, he wanted to proceed with this charade he calls a therapeutic strategy. Not one of his multi-layered questions elicits a response. No matter how he put it, Languid wouldn't give it. Not a word. But the resourceful Dr Churr didn't stop there; if he couldn't get the evidence of the abuse through words then he would ask him to delve back into earlier childhood and artistically explore these memories. No joy there either. Without a tangible response to hang his theory on, this so-called therapist didn't want to have his ideas seen to be undermined, not with another publishing deal in the

. . . .

131

pipeline and some cable *Get Shrunk* shows in the offing, and so he made it clear to all concerned that denial was evidence of abuse itself.

Jesus, Sad, any memories I might have of fisting sequentially my parent's fifteen cats is just malicious gossip and I'll sue, okay?

Anyway the parents were pretty uneasy about all of this – they had a healthy, conservative distrust of recovered memory therapy, viewed it as some Bohemian replacement to religion, where there was no God and no moral structure. *Kneejerk Oprah, how to fake with Rikki Lake . . .* And when this guy tried to localise the cause of Languid's mute demeanour, by suggesting with the deftness of a drunken ballerina that at some point something may have shocked him enough to stun him into silence, something for instance like an unexpected finger in an unexpected place . . . well . . . Even when Languid's parents were telling me this, they hit the roof, so God help the guy when they discovered he was trying to infer sexual abuse from his silence. They probably would have had a contract put out on him for even thinking it never mind trying to pry it out of him with blunt pencils and a piece of paper.

But you know me, Sad, I'd be the first to stand up at an international therapists' conference, my plastic ID badge swinging in an air thick with bullshit, and say that yes sexual abuse does exist. Christ, I'd do a standup, toe-tapping routine if that's what it takes, but Languid's parents weren't abusers, at least not in the sexual arena. Other ways certainly – from routine hits for sense to come rushing back in to periods locked in his room – '*and don't come out until you have something to say*' – but *they* into his adolescent lingerie? They just weren't the types.

In their own way Languid's parents had scaled down their expectations of what they themselves could get

. . . .

from their son. There was an ideal at the beginning that interaction was what they wanted from him, but as months turned into years without a peep out of him they reduced their expectations to simply getting a *reaction* from their son. As I've told you they were middle-of-the-road tending to the right sort of people and not the sort to settle down to an evening of violent films with everybody from Van Damme to Willis filling their exclusive suburban setting with Uzzi ricochets, but that's exactly what they did, hoping that their popcorn-munching son would imitate the set-pieces and start kicking shit out of the dog. At the very least they hoped that they might get some colourful expletives. But nothing. Then the father confided to me, when his wife was away wiping Languid's nose unnecessarily, that he had rented a few soft-porn videos for the boy in the hope that curiosity or embarrassment might encourage speech of some sort. Nothing. Not even a furtive, soggy wank behind the sofa, not an *Oh, ah* breathlessly whispered. The last thing they had tried themselves before moving into uncharted therapy waters was leaving him in the middle of a village square while vacationing in Provence, France. They ditched him after some deliberate shopping confusion and then proceeded to watch Languid from their hotel bedroom sauntering around looking for his parents, eating a few ice creams and staring a lot at the sky. It wasn't the reaction they had wanted. They had thought maybe he would freak and run to some hapless gendarme and cry for his mother and father, the fear of being left alone in a foreign town suddenly bursting his verbal dam. Nothing.

This was a boy who had decided not to talk. At some point, for some reason. A dreamboat of a case that had many of my fellow hacks falling over themselves to get a shot at it. Guess I'm the lucky one, eh, Sad?

FAX POSTCARD 2

Still waiting for Stretch and Wait to arrive with the goodies, trying not to pace the cabin floor or give in too much to results panic. Christ, even a minute ago there I was thinking I'd better get something conventional going here and start a little card game – now is that a vase or two people French kissing . . .? Save me from that, save him from that! I've got a cutting-edge reputation to keep for Christ's sake. I needed to get some air, needed to rejuvenate my confidence with some serious O_2. Much as I hate to admit it, much as I'd like to take some years back and find Stretch, Wait and myself buzzing on something without a care in our student world, I've got to face up to some responsibilities here. Know what I'm saying? If this doesn't work out I'm going to have the parents, the grant board, the Institute on my back for wasting precious resources and building up false hopes – the fucks, they'd rather have the false memories . . . Worse still, there's plenty of up-and-comings back in the office who would love me to take a fall, take a trip to some professional nowhere.

Pathetic, Sad, I know, but you've got to ditch the negative and build up the positive and I guess that's why you're getting this. This is dangerous territory here, there are no stepping stones, no half-measures – at least not for Languid. Everybody's pussyfooted around him for long enough, from his doting mother to the dotty quacks and somebody, meaning yours truly, has to take a stand and put the psyche back into psychotherapy. No one's interested, are they, Sad? No one's fucking interested in getting to the nitty-gritty any more, cutting to the chase and all that. The state of potted plants in some padded office has become more important than the development of strategies to treat those deeply reactive to our lifetimes.

. . . .

Yeah, I know, it's soapbox jury again and you're worrying about the trees and your budget as I eat up the paper in your fax machine but really, it just makes my blood boil, makes me crazy but not in the institutional sense.

With that, it's enough to say that we left a note for Stretch and Wait on the door and strode out the cabin about eight hours ago and just got back.

It wasn't exactly a journey into the heart of darkness, nothing was defined or solved in those eight hours, but it was good for me to work on my treading-water technique, relearning that patience is what this is about and I guess out here patience should come naturally. We must have made quite a pair if anyone had been around to see us. Ageing thirtysomething losing his hair and gaining some waist accompanied by this thin as a rake, insipid blond mouse. I could see why the parents wanted him to talk, to live their social life and dreams, because in all other respects he fitted the bill. He had that aristocratic look about him that would no doubt send his fellow pubescent whoevers wild. I liked him. I liked him enough to try and find a way of communicating with him that didn't rely on words. In the same vein, I liked him enough to place him fairly and squarely at the forefront of experimental drug psychotherapy.

He would thank me one day.

I tried out a few clichés on him, not to insult his intelligence but to eradicate the need for the clichés themselves. Besides, no one was going to back my radical results unless some humdrum controls were done. I joked for the first hour with him, played the fool and revisited my childhood just for him. I told him

....

about how I used to shin up trees with the greatest of ease, like a hairless monkey stuck on bark and often day after day in some distant summer my parents would find me up some tree whenever we went near more than a clump of them. I loved the challenge, the fear, the excitement, and even when I got stuck the desire to continue never drained. Later on, along with Stretch and Wait, at college I swung on a few branches, tripping out so that from trunk to trunk, branch to branch in some urban wood became vine after vine in a throbbing jungle.

In the here and now I did it again just for him and maybe a bit for me. I clambered up some average-size tree with less athleticism but with no less enjoyment from earlier days and I fooled about trying to get him to join in. But he gave me that look that got him his name, he just kind of smiled and looked at the scenery as I huffed and puffed, twigs spiking my cheeks.

Then I took it a step further and suggested we cross the rapids rather than walk for miles trying to find a bridge or a safer place to cross. I could tell that he disagreed and that in itself was an accomplishment, not because he knew there must be a less dangerous place to cross than the place I was suggesting – any half-wit could see the white water was trouble – but of course that isn't the point. The point is that I knew that he disagreed without a word being spoken. It was, as they say, Sad, in the eyes. This is the start of the theory, that communication comes in many shapes and forms and if this could be transferred to a hallucinogenic situation then there could be a torrent of dreams, hates, desires coming forth. Fuck knows what, but somewhere in that jumble of ideas and reactions there might, just might, be room for words to tell his story. Gone would be the Languid stare.

....

I held my own in the water, kept my feet planted on the river bed and I could have made it across the stretch of water but I thought that would defeat the purpose so I lost my footing, stumbled and went under. At this point I had to focus my attention away from my cliché scheme of getting him to come to my rescue – like a post-traumatic stress Lassie, and suddenly he would emerge out of his shell with a new and whole purpose – and concentrate on not losing my footing for real. The pull of the current was quite strong and the thought did cross my mind that if his parents were here and saw the potential danger, I would be in deep shit with a malpractice suit as high as the mountains slammed into my face. Probably worse would be the field day my colleagues would have with my field experiment. At best I would be a fool in their eyes, taking unnecessary risks with a sensitive patient, glamorising danger with the kind of foolhardy technique that gives psychotherapy a bad name. At worst I was an old hippie desperately trying to find an academic slant to what was little more than narcotic addiction.

Anyhow, I went under a few times to add some drama to the situation plus a bit of coughing and spluttering for effect and each time I came up I watched for signs from him. But, Jesus, Sad, I swear if I'd let go of the rock in my hands and went floating off downriver like a fucking log he would have just stood there, that look, that indecipherable, impenetrable look on his face. Not that I hold it against him. He's been through enough therapists and psychs to know that we all play games in order to make people realise that they are playing games with themselves and so maybe he knew what it was all about. He could simply have seen through my dramatic ploy or possibly he didn't care what happened to the pseudo-suit who had taken him out into the country away from his nice home. I don't

....

know. Perhaps it was an exercise in the fruitless, but as you know, Sad, you got to clean the wall before you paint it, you've got to get a hard-on before you can fuck . . . catch the drift? It was worth getting wet just to eliminate the obvious.

FAX POSTCARD 3

Stretch and Wait have arrived. Couriers of cutting-edge psychiatric treatment. The first thing Stretch tells me, as he flakes out in front of the fire Languid is building with studied concentration, is that our psychohack colleague and stimulant supplier has been busted. Not in the criminal sense but in the professional breakdown sense. Seems that he'd got away from the psychedelics that had us all knocking on heaven's door ten years back when we were undergraduates together in a brown-wallpaper flat and walked into a coke habit. Stupid fuck, we all agree. What's the point? Bad drug, inane chatter and short duration. It was all too ironic. The guy, Sense, as he was called on account of his big ears and acute listening skills, worked at an up-market detox centre for downwardly mobile stars of yesterday, counselling and cajoling them out of their sad fucking habits. *Do you want to see your name up in lights again? Then give me your stash.* You know the sort of thing, the kind of sting operated in clubs and police stations the length and breadth of the country. Chastise and confiscate, classify and use. Guess they had some pretty rich clientele at the place if it was Charlie that got him. The short and not so sweet of it was that the sickness days started to accumulate, the distrust of friends grew and soon paranoia was in its roost. Stretch says that when he went to pick up the acid, Sense was beside himself, first tears then fisticuffs while in between tirades he would watch the windows and talk about how he needed help. Can you believe it, Sad, a psycho-

....

hack asking for help? You truly know when the bottom of the barrel has been scraped. It has a gritty sound to it, an earthy smell to it.

What do we care anyway? Wait says he knows another guy, in the local nuthouse, who can take care of our occasional recreational needs. Temperance mixed with hedonism is the only way to survive in these days of extremes. And here we are wishing you were here to join us with some of your witty parlour talk and pithy songs, making do with the three of us and little Languid, so quiet, so fragile, so open to our charms.

Hey, Sad, you are burning these faxes aren't you?
  Just joking.
  Not.

Stretch and Wait. Queer as fuck. Once matching T-shirts, now matching incomes. Stretch counsels the bereaved of whatever hue, recovering from the sudden or protracted death of a loved one. Wait rakes it in counselling sperm-free men and ovary-dented women. Not marriage counselling, he insists, but *Relationship Retrieval*. Can you believe it? He's up his own ass with jargon as much as the wall-bangers back at the Institute. Can't say I like him much, which is a terrible thing to admit considering how long I've known him, but it's Stretch I've always connected with. He got me into acid, got me into the periphery of counterculture and took me on some mad trips into mountains not unlike these. Heady days indeed but Wait always brought an edge to our otherwise flawless delirium. If we were in danger of becoming embroiled in a world of caftans and batiks, he'd slip on some John Cale or John Cage and weird us out, all the time his beady eyes staring at us expectantly hoping for some sign of awe or at least

....

respect. Somehow, sometime they hooked up together and became an item. 'Take Stretch and you've gotta Wait', was what people said. Now look at them. Now look at all of us. Three psychohacks trading on half-assed qualifications rejuvenating our hedonism as much as our professionalism will allow.

I love it.

Languid must be wondering what the hell is going on. He might have had an inkling of what to expect when his parents told him he was going on a weekend break with a psychotherapist to help him break out of his wall of silence and then he might have had another idea when he met me and we went striding around the countryside in pursuit of something. But now with Stretch and Wait here – Stretch opening up a wrap with ten square Barts while Wait slinks around hovering near Languid as he warms his hands by the fire – his preconceptions will be at best confused. If I was him I would be terrified. But then I was meek and mousy at his age without the resilience he has shown. His parents are wrong when they think it is some kind of genetic weakness that he is the way he is in his silent world. To be like that takes strength. But that's the attraction as you well know, Sad. Wasn't it Stang that said, *We all find the world of the delusional attractive for in that world they can reinvent themselves in a way we can only do in our dreams*?

Don't you just hate it when they get it right?

Meanwhile, as I wax lyrical, or type awkwardly to be accurate, Stretch is furrowing his brow trying to work out the scenario beyond the bare details I had given him. In the mountains. One patient. Both need invigoration. Come now, the fax postcard had read. The cryptic message had got him here but he is uncertain as to

....

Languid's role, no doubt surprised how young he is, no doubt perturbed that Wait is going to be distracted for the duration. Two shrinks, a child and a chicken hawk. Some combination.

He put his palm over the acid.

'Will he talk?'

'Shit, I hope so,' I told him.

I filled them both in quickly, out of earshot of Languid. Stretch nodded while Wait's eyes lit up. No doubt a sense of opportunity was flickering through his mind, a warm feeling filling his stem.

'I could make him talk.'

I told him, 'How many times have I heard that before? How many times has he heard it before?'

'Making him scream doesn't count, dear,' Stretch said.

Can't say I was rippling with laughter at that one. Languid's kind of under my care and the last thing I want is Wait testing his oral threshold for pain. But it's noted and Wait will behave himself. We're all friends here just wanting to push out the boat for a few hours, nothing more, nothing less.

This is what I have to tell you, and you might not jump over the moon about it, you might even reach for the phone or a gun. What can I say? Therapy not just friendship should dare to risk. I've left all my blunt devices back in the city, all those tired old theories about counselling him into speech, rooting out original causes for his silence. This is the Delong Mountains, Alaska, and I can't think of a better place for a cutting edge.

We're going to gulp these squares, two for the adults and one for the boy. And maybe you won't want to read the next bulletin, Sad, I don't know, I really don't

....

know. Will I have to explain the difference between putting a tab in a stranger's drink down the local then watching him wrestle with pool sticks and ogle moose heads and our Languid, a world of voice sucked out of him by timidity and control? If I have to explain it or if you are professionally revolted then get the shredder ready is all I can say.

FAX POSTCARD 4

I pulled a fast one about six hours ago and it was one of my better moves. Guess it's not kosher really, not really adhering to the unspoken rituals of drug circles whether they are in mansions or cubicles, *pass the dutchie on the left hand side . . . third light is bad luck . . . don't bogart that joint my friend . . .*, but I only took half while I watched Stretch and Wait tan their two tabs. Seeing the situation as I do now – and even with a half still in my system it's still difficult to see anything in the traditional sense – I needed to have some grip on where I am and why, while all around me everybody else lost theirs. For Languid, especially for Languid. Wait made him a cup of adulterated coffee just after he had set the fire and he drunk it as he sat at the table watching the light being sucked from the sky. He was wary of both of them and while he hadn't exactly warmed to me during our brief time together there was a quiet sense of something between us and I guessed – and I admit I could be wide of the mark, teeing up my own sense of psychohack ego – that he was in his own way relaxed with me. Not that he was about to talk a mile a minute, but in the subtleties of unspoken communication there was something going on. But this kind of took a back seat when Stretch and Wait arrived and although Languid is far from streetwise, cocooned as he has been for most of his privileged life, he cannot have failed to feel Wait's eyes, ripping the shirt off his

. . . .

back, pulling his jeans down . . . Before the acid took hold Wait was content to hang around Languid, patting his shoulder reassuringly, squeezing himself close to him as he sat at the table, constantly talking under his breath to him as though *sotto voce*, half-said, trailing-off sentences was his technique for making Languid shout out with frustration.

Stretch wasn't interested in hearing Languid talk. It wasn't his problem. He was taking some R & R and all he wanted was to ease himself into a hallucinatory state while slugging back a few beers talking about old times and new theories – he was used to his partner ogling chicken, it was part and parcel of their relationship and while he didn't share his predilections he wasn't about to rein in Wait's desires.

For Stretch and Wait this was another weekend of hedonism which they occasionally indulged in with me but routinely with each other. For me this was still a working weekend with a job to do and an outcome to be achieved but, as the acid took hold and started knotting my stomach and shivering my vision, I was going to need the control just taking a half afforded me. Call me sentimental, call me a workaholic, describe me as unable to relax but I wanted to be there for Languid once his coffee had been drunk. Guess you might call it guilt for setting up this whole situation in the first place but I was just nervous for him, that's all. The guy would have eventually been pumped full of some kind of prescriptive drug anyway – his parents had threatened as much, having exhausted most holistic and video-based approaches – and if he was going to take something to take him out of himself (now where have I heard that before . . .?) then it might as well be the granddaddy of escapism.

He was the first to move under the influence. While

. . . .

143

Stretch and Wait gripped the table, their legs shaking, heads rolling from one side to another in some kind of time to the music I'd brought with me, Languid suddenly stood up and started to walk around the perimeter of the room. Our eyes followed him, a sudden entertainment for our rushing heads, as he shifted furniture out of his way so he could circumnavigate the room without interruption. There was a determined look on his pale face, his tongue slipping between his teeth in a grimace that showed neither pain nor pleasure. I felt relieved at this. No one could have been sure how he would have reacted to being spiked. I guess in my head I had simplified his reaction into *What the fuck is going on*? and that this sudden spouting of concern and confusion would have been his first taste of oral communication which, once he had been reassured and calmed, would have then led to conversations, reactions, in other words interaction that was the goal of our trip to the mountains. This was the theory in action, the half-cocked, half-baked idea that I had drummed up, that served the very essence of what I believe. Unconventional therapies. Unproved theories.

I hadn't allowed for Wait in the scheme of things.

He fell off his chair and started to gyrate like a sheep stuck in mud. I think he was laughing but his voice sounded so contorted that it was difficult to tell. Stretch's head was down on the table, his hands clasped over his ears, shutting out some soundless cacophony, and in my semi-delirious state I observed the irony of that. Wait had fallen into the path of Languid's circuit, a threshing machine of stubby limbs, a lump of unkempt and deteriorating flesh . . . and Languid at first simply jumped over him with an agility and ease of

. . . .

movement that I envied but after a particularly quick circuit, just as he jumped, Wait stretched out a hand and brought him down unceremoniously. I heard Languid's head hit the floorboards and the sound was sickening.

If I had been stone cold I would have dealt with the situation with concern but pragmatically; if I had been totally wrecked I would gibbered some remark about fallen angels in a heathen world and lost my self to images of white doves being shot down over an Arctic landscape – you get the idea anyway, Sad. As it was I just got paranoid. I thought of head injuries, permanent scars and law suits. I started a conversation in my head trying to break the news to Languid's parents about the tragic accident that led to his death. This, Sad, was and is a sign of the times. Ten years ago in our brown-wallpaper flat, paranoia and reality concern would not have been part of the experience – *we were young . . . with nothing to lose.*

Wait wouldn't let Languid up. As they grappled, Languid's face was expressionless as always, his eyes fixed on something on the ceiling. All Wait's eyes were fixed on was the trickle of blood coming from a small cut on Languid's forehead. He climbed up the boy's body as though he was hanging on to some steep cliff face and his chubby face pressed into Languid's thick jumper. He was losing it, I thought, but I was rooted to the spot by something, the half acid, the half-assed attempt to get out of it. And Stretch just wasn't in the picture. He was still folded in on himself.

There should be a sense of freedom here, I kept thinking.

Wait's once cherubic now simply fat face bulged over Languid and his tongue darted out to the cut, its twin trickles of blood streaking down the whiter than white

. . . .

skin. In my head it was getting worse. A gargoyle was clambering over a sleeping princess, a scarab beetle was crawling over white desert sand ... Anyway, the result was that I shut my eyes, not willing to see or intervene and the next thing I knew, the next thing I heard was a sharp, high-pitched cry of pain. I opened my eyes to see trails of blues and reds darting across the floor following Wait as he rolled from side to side clenching his genitals. Languid jumped up and walked slowly out the door. Finally, Stretch raised his head and mumbled what sounded like, 'What happened?'

It wasn't hard to work out. Wait had no doubt expected no resistance from Languid and had been reminded that it was best to expect the unexpected when it came to tripping.

Well, as you can imagine, Sad, my half-cut neuroses got fully fledged. It was pulse-racing stuff but way off the mark from what I had hoped for. The phrase *it's all going horribly wrong* was ringing gothically in my head while for some reason Jack Nicholson was coming out the wall with an axe in his hand. I had to find a grip of some sort and I was not going to get any help from my colleagues. Stretch was gradually surfacing from his stupor but managed only to clamber out of his seat onto the table to inspect with ridiculous fervour the beer bottle tipped on its side slowly dripping the remains of its contents onto a postcard he had started to write earlier. Wait had managed to crawl on all fours to the fire and seemed to find some kind of solace in the glowing embers. My first and most rational thought since the acid took hold was fuck 'em. We were not the most collaborative of trippers – psycho-hacks never are, I'm told – all that education and training and fine words go out the window and we become the worst of patients, the most self-absorbed of trippers. Back in college days each one of us could

....

146

have tried to step off some high building to traverse some astral plain and the others would have been picking fluff out of their buttons. It always seems to take a trip to remind me of that.

I went after Languid. It was a familiar walk, not because of the location but because of the sensation. All three of us had trooped on various occasions out of the safe environment of our brown-wallpapered walls into the outside world. A visit to the grocery or liquor store became an adventure that could send us into inane giggling fits or disabling paranoia. Stretch took what seemed like an hour to walk from our flat to the pavement outside. He was putting one foot firmly in front of the other, the kind of heel-toe shuffle that would have seen him in the store about five hours later if he'd kept it.

'Why are you walking like that?' Wait had asked him.

'In case I lose my balance and fall.'

'Fall into what?' he was asked.

'Don't you see the cracks? God knows what would happen if I stepped on one . . .'

That old children's game of avoid the cracks had become a game of chance, a matter of life and death in our tripping eyes. There was always laughter in the end, our ridiculous behaviour became the point rather than any particular variety of mind expansion. But there was no laughter now. Stretch and Wait had folded and if it had not been for Languid I would have joined them to complete the sorry sight.

Languid was nowhere to be seen. My eyesight was still in the throes of distortion but it was calming down and again I reminded myself that I had been sensible not to swallow the two tabs that had Stretch and Wait

....

prostrate. Sensible, I hear you coughing into your pillow, Sensible? Sensible would never have got into a situation like this, would never have attempted to crossbreed the professional with the psychoactive but then this was truly a case of nothing ventured nothing gained. Languid had nothing to lose, I kept telling myself as I searched around the dark perimeter of the cabin, his silence would have been battered out of him one way or another.

I'm not sure how long I looked for him, long enough for some light to be seen on the horizon, long enough for me to make up a headline to be read by my superiors and founders ... *experiment in the mountains goes horribly wrong, drug-crazed therapists attack and molest young boy in hallucinatory frenzy* ...

I didn't find Languid; he found me. I was at the point of deciding he must have fallen down one of the steep hills leading away from the cabin, skittered down some scree into gorse bushes and was now lying a scarred and twisted mess. I put no trust in his ability to survive the whirling maelstrom of a spiked head and even less in mine to be able to deal with it. As it was I felt a hand reach out and grab my shoulder and while I jumped ten feet in the air with fright Languid turned me around so that when I landed my face was pressed close to his. Even though the light was slipping into our mountain world it was still too dark for me to see Languid's face clearly but I saw a riot of expression and colour. His pale skin had been smeared with his own blood mixed with dust from the open fire and earth from outside the cabin. His pupils were dilated and a smile ripped across his face. He was far from the distraught, pining figure I had expected him to be. He pulled me closer to him, so that our noses almost touched. He must have seen the startled look on my face, the unprofessional look of personal concern. He

....

patted my cheek with the palm of his hand and said two words, 'Good acid.' With that he picked up an axe lying at his feet and went off to chop more wood for the fire.

He left me speechless. Inside the cabin. Stretch was back into his pre-acid position, holding a bottle of beer, rubbing the label absentmindedly with his fingers. He raised the bottle when I came in and said two words:

'Good acid.'

Wait looked as though he was sleeping, his small stocky body curled up next to the fire, his breath heavy, his hands fidgeting and scratching at his legs as he held them close to his chest.

He looked up from the floor as I walked past him.

'Good acid,' he said hoarsely.

I sat down in the kitchen, well away from the two of them, and began to write my report to Languid's parents.

It may simply be the case that your son will only talk when he has something to say . . .

Victor Spoils

(from 'The Gricers', a work in regress)

IRVINE WELSH

She should be enjoying herself.

The light blue wall, the back of the old brown corduroy settee in front of her, her elbows on its cushions and him behind her, his large hands not that far from circling her entire waist. His prick inside her, moving in a strange insistent rhythm, and his encouraging sounds.

Sarah's thinking that she should be enjoying herself.

She should be enjoying herself but she most certainly isn't. When she thinks why, Sarah reckons that it could be because it's too cold to be naked. But that shouldn't be an issue, and it wouldn't be an issue, not if her tooth wasn't hurting. Now she is feeling self-conscious, aware of herself on this couch, sprawled out in front of Gavin, like an extension of his prick, and the whole point of sex is not to feel self-conscious. It's difficult though, when your tooth is hurting and you're the recipient of Gavin's Hollywood-style seduction techniques, so obviously gleaned from the sections in formula videos when the music changes and the leading couple get on it. First, the foreplay; second, the penetration; third, the positions; fourth, the orgasm (simultaneous of course). When Gavin mumbles 'You're gorgeous' or 'You've got a great body' Sarah imagines that she should be flattered, but this is done with the concentrated detachment of a wooden actor trying to remember his lines.

Gavin hopes that the sheer force of ceremony and ritual, the expression of the appropriate word and gesture, is going to weave together a smart, nice-fitting suit which will take pride of place in that wardrobe crammed with his life's social fabric. While he is imaginative enough, Gavin knows that he possesses the exclusive imagination of the only child amusing himself quietly by setting up armies of soldiers for battle on the carpet and that this training had not given him the essential speed of thought to enable him to make contingency plans if anything went amiss in his almost psychologically story-boarded seduction routine.

In the club that night he had been full of Ecstasy, which always helped. Gavin had made the point of kissing every girl in the company (which on this particular night meant every girl in the club) but with Sarah he'd slipped a bit of tongue into her mouth, soul into his eyes and let his hand linger in the small of her back where it seemed determined to set up residence.

To Sarah, such attentions were a welcome source of affirmation since her split from Victor. She'd recently grown half-aware that guys were mistaking her pissed-off look for the less ambiguous 'keep-the-fuck-away-from-me' variety. So as clubbers danced under the flashing lights and the loudspeaker pumped the latest throbbing bass lines through their bodies, Gavin and Sarah found themselves in an embrace as welcoming as it was surprising.

Gavin was entranced by the fluid suggestiveness of Sarah's eyes and the mesmerising movement of her

....

151

red-glossed lips as she spoke. She, in turn, was surprised at how much she fancied Gavin – his big soulful eyes, his easy if slightly cheesy grin – simply because she had always disliked him when he was with Lynda.

That night she had enjoyed his touch. Although often intimate, it had no sense of the sewer in it. She reciprocated by giving him a massage, starting off by gently stroking the tendons of his neck, then increasing with an imperceptible force to knead the MDMA through his body until it pulsed like a beautiful open wound.

They evacuated into the early morning chill and took a taxi to his place, where they sat up hugging, kissing and talking, removing articles of clothing as they went, losing themselves in long, shared journeys as they snogged. Gavin explained that penetrative sex would be out of the question for a while, which Sarah felt less than chuffed about, but accepted. Later, with the MDMA running down and the tiredness settling into their bodies, they fell into a comatose sleep on the couch in front of the gas fire.

Sarah awoke to Gavin's caresses. Her body immediately responded but something was not right in her head. This was now post-MDMA, another set of circumstances, and Gavin, she feels, hasn't acknowledged this. She does want to start all over again, but she doesn't want Gavin to make some kind of affirmation that things are now different and terms have to be restated as much as renegotiated. And her toothache. She thought it had left her alone, this wisdom tooth problem. But these things never went away, you just got a bit of remission.

And now it was back.

It was back all right, and with such a persistent, spiteful vengeance as to suggest the same malevolent,

....

mean-spirited force which had drawn up and implemented the Criminal Justice Bill.

Gavin had woken with his cock stiff and throbbing. He pulled the duvet cover from them, at first mildly surprised at his and Sarah's nakedness. Then he drew a deep breath and felt a surge of wonder rise in him. It was like winning the lottery. Then mild paranoia that his inarticulacy and arousal would take off on different tangents settled into his psyche. It had to happen, and it had to happen now, otherwise she would think there was something weird about him. He had to show her a good time as well, especially after all the things they had said last night. The way he hadn't been able to go for it, in a penetrative sense, and was there really any other? he considered, the thought disturbing him slightly. He knew that women liked guys who had imagination and who could use their tongues and their fingers, but at the end of the day they still wanted to be fucked and he hadn't been able to deliver the goods last night. Yes, he had to show her a good time. That was crucial. Gavin's tongue ripped his dry lips apart as he felt consciousness submerge and movement take over as his hands glided towards her.

So it was that Sarah felt herself being bent and moved like a mechanical doll while Gavin thrust himself into her from all different angles, all the time with his accompanying banal bleatings which jarred at any sense of abandon. Worse, every time she threatened to get into it and just seemed to be transcending the pain of her toothache, he would stop, withdraw and change positions like an assembly worker on job rotation. At one point she wanted to scream with frustration. To her surprise, they did achieve something close to simultaneous orgasm, her coming first and Gavin *just* after, her thrashings against him, against the toothache,

....

against the frustrations of the situation, telling him — Don't fuckin move and don't fuckin come!

Gavin dug in, thinking that it would be a brave man who did either in face of such ferocity as she brought herself off against him.

So while the eventual destination was satisfactory, the nagging toothache prevented Sarah from basking in the afterglow and forced her to reflect that she wasn't sure whether she wanted to make this particular kind of trip in Gavin's company again.

She twisted and writhed in his proprietary arms, then pulled away and sat up on the couch.

—What is it? he moaned in a drowsy petulance, like a child confronted by a bigger kid who had designs on his sweets.

Sarah put her hand to her jaw, and let her tongue probe the back of her mouth. A spasm of sharp pain shot through the omnipresent dull ache. — Mmm . . . she groaned.

—Eh? Gavin prompted, his eyes widening.

—I've got toothache, she said. It hurt to talk, but as soon as she stated this, she realised that it was unbearable.

—Want a paracetamol?

—Ah want a fuckin dentist! she snapped through the agony, holding her jaw to support that effort. That was the worst thing about pain of this sort: it seemed to draw strength from the first acknowledgement of how bad it was. Now it was getting as bad as she could imagine pain getting.

—Aye, eh . . . right . . . Gavin stood up. The toothache, he remembered, she had mentioned it last night. It was okay then, but it must be kicking in now. — I'll see if ah kin git a number. It'll need tae be one ay the emergency punters this being a Sunday n that.

—I just need a dentist, she howled.

. . . .

Gavin sat down on a chair and started thumbing through a Thomson's Local. There was a tatty note pad with numbers and doodlings on it. He had put a thick box round the bold lettering FEED SPARKY. His mother's cat. He said he would. The poor thing was probably starving.

He found a number in the Thomson's Local and dialled it. The book flipped shut. The cat on the cover picture of the directory seemed to judge him on Sparky's behalf.

Then there was a voice on the end of the line.

He looked strange, just sitting there naked, Sarah thought, talking on the phone to a dentist or a receptionist. His circumcised cock. The first time she had ever done it with a guy with a circumcised cock, the first time she had ever *seen* a circumcised cock. She wanted to ask him why he had got it done. Religious reasons? Medical ones? Hygiene? Sexual? They said that women enjoyed sex with circumcised cocks, but it hadn't felt different to her. She would ask

a spasm of pain
the fuckin pain

Gavin still talking on the phone

—Yes it is an emergency. No way can it wait.

Sarah looked up and felt good about Gavin, his positiveness, his lack of wavering, his resolute putting of her needs first in this situation. She tried to flash some sort of message of gratitude, but her gaze didn't catch his eye and her hair fell over her face.

—Right, that's twenty-five Drumsheugh Gardens. Twelve o'clock. Is that as soon as ye kin manage? Okay . . . Right, thank you. He put the phone down and looked up at her. — They kin take ye in an hour, doon the New Town. It wis the quickest the guy oan

....

call could git oot tae the surgery. If we head off now, we can stop at Mulligan's fir a drink. Dae ye think ye could swallay a paracetemol?

—I don't know . . . aye, ah could.

—Ye swallayed enough pills last night, Gavin laughed.

Sarah tried to smile, but it hurt too much. She did, however, managed to swallow a pill and they made their way down the road, Sarah moving in grim deliberation, Gavin in a tense symbiosis.

The bright autumn sun nipped their eyes as they walked down Cockburn Street. Gavin looked at the sign, Cockburn Street. Though it was pronounced Cobirn, Gavin felt a rawness in his genitals. Cockburn, right enough. He looked at Sarah, she had taken her hand from her face. She was fuckin lovely, sure she was. He didn't even want to look at her tits or her arse or anything although they were fuckin beautiful, as he'd seen last night, but now they were just swamped by the essence of her. When you can only feel the essence, not visualise the constituent parts, Gavin considered, that's when you know that you are falling in love. Fuck. When did it happen? Maybe when he was on the phone. You could never tell with these things! Fuckin hell. Sarah!

Sarah.

He wanted to take care of her, help her through this. Just be there with her. For her.

Gavin 4 Sarah.

Maybe he should hold her hand. But he was jumping ahead of himself. God, he'd just fucked her every way! Why couldn't he hold her hand? What was wrong with this fucking world, how had we come to get so perverse that holding the hand of a lassie you were in love with was a heavier deal than shagging her doggy style across your settee?

And what was he doing saying that they'd go to

Mulligan's? The whole posse would be there, carrying on, keeping it going, some of them doing more pills. A few had probably been in the Boundary Bar since five this morning. Gavin tried to distance himself from a growing feeling of unease by loftily considering that he had all the chemicals he needed, the natural chemicals of love. The self-loathing was growing though. It wouldn't go away. It was like her toothache. Was he really such a bastard that he wanted to parade her like a trophy in Mulligan's. I FUCKED SARAH McWILLIAMS LAST NIGHT. No, it hadn't been like that, he'd wanted the world to know that they were, as they say, an item. But were they? What did she think?

Maybe he should just take her hand, just do it.

Sarah thought *dentist dentist dentist*. The steps that had to be taken, the streets that had to be crossed, to narrow that terrifying distance between pain and treatment. There was one bad, traffic-infested roundabout in the way. Her heart felt heavy. She didn't know if she could do it, cross over that roundabout. The cars seemed to slow down and speed up, play a cat-and-mouse game with you, dare you to try and cross. But they were over. Then there was Princess Street first, then Mulligan's. She couldn't go to Mulligan's! What the fuck was he thinking about? But Louise and Julia would be there. They'd chum her. Yes, Mulligan's.

Then she felt him grab her hand. What was he doing?

—Ye okay? he asked, concern scribbled on his face in the broad strokes of a crayon in an infant's fist. Expressions of sincerity were something she always found painful in men she didn't know that well. There was something so obvious about Gavin, so overplayed, not so much that of a person who was false as of one who had never learned to be comfortable being real and

....

157

AGHHHH

Then a bigger spasm of pain, of *real* pain and her squeezing on his hand.

—It's okay, we'll be there soon. Yir really suffering, eh? Gavin asked. Of course she was. He should shut up. Inappropriate, that was him, everything about him. His friends were inappropriate. He never saw Renton now, nobody did, nor much of Begbie, thank the heavens, or Sick Boy or Nelly or Spud or Second Prize but they were inappropriate. Higher Executive Officers in the Department of Employment did not have friends like that. Executive Officers did at one time, before they find their limits, but HEOs have never had friends like that. No HEO ever had a pal like Spud Murphy. He would never be an HEO because he was tainted by an association with people he now seldom saw. This manifested itself by drinking too much, coming in obviously cunted on a Monday. It was Tuesday that really did you though. You go through the Monday still on a bit of a high, but the comedown always kicked in on the Tuesday. And they noticed. They had to have noticed, over the years. Thus no HEO. Perhaps he shouldn't have stayed a weekend waster. Perhaps he should have gone full-time, he thought bitterly.

Sarah hadn't even bothered trying to respond because this was hell and it couldn't get any worse but it *was* getting worse, much worse because she sensed a presence. Sensed it before she saw it. It was him.

Sarah looked up as they crossed over Market Street, because Victor was coming towards them. His face, pinched and hard, his classical self-absorbed look, which broke up into one of disbelief, then outrage, as he registered them coming towards him hand in hand.

Gavin saw him too. But it was over, her and Victor,

....

and he'd have to know about it sooner or later. He liked Victor; they were mates. They'd drank together, partied together, gone to the fitba together. Always in company, mind you, never just the two of them on their own, but they'd done it for long enough over the years for them to be more than just acquaintances. And Gavin liked him, he really did. He knew that Vic was what his Dad would call a man's man, which he supposed was a sort of euphemism by omission for maybe not the type of guy a lassie would get much joy from in a relationship. But Gavin liked him. Vic had to know about him and Sarah, he had to know some time. Gavin wished that it could be later, but it wasn't to be.

—Awright, Victor said, his hands resting on his hips.

—Vic, Gavin nodded. He looked at Sarah, then back at Victor, who was still in the gunfighter stance.

Sarah just looked away.

—Oot last night? Gavin asked tepidly.

—See you wir, aye, Victor looked Gavin scornfully up and down, then turned to Sarah. His hateful gaze burned her so much that for a moment she forgot her toothache.

—Ah've goat nowt tae say tae you, she mumbled.

—Mibbee ah've goat something tae say tae you!

—Vic look, Gavin said, — we've goat tae git tae the dentist . . .

—You shut yir fuckin mooth lover boy! Victor pointed at Gavin, who felt the blood draining from his face. — Ah'll knock yir fuckin teeth oot then yi'll huv tae go tae the fuckin dentist awright!

The fear rose within. Yet a part of his mind was working coldly, detached from what was going on around him. He thought that he should assault Victor first, in order to prevent Vic from hitting him. Yet he felt guilt towards Victor. And there was the self-preservation instinct. Would he be able to take Victor?

Doubtful, but the outcome hardly mattered. What would Sarah want, that was the question. The dentist. They had to get to the dentist.

—That's your answer tae everything, eh! Sarah said, screwing up her eyes and nose.

—How long's this been gaun oan? Eh? How long ye been seein that cunt!? Victor demanded.

—Its none ay your fuckin business what ah dae!

—How fuckin long? Victor roared, lunging forward, grabbing her by the arm and shaking her.

Gavin sprang forward and smacked Victor in the jaw. Victor's head jerked back as Gavin tensed, ready to follow up. Victor put one hand to his face and raised his other, signalling for Gavin to back away. Blood spilled in droplets onto the pavement from his wound.

—Sorry Vic . . . sorry man, but ye shouldnae've done that eh . . . sorry but man . . . Gavin felt confused. He'd hit Victor. His mate. He'd fucked his mate's bird, and then he had panelled the boy for being upset. That was out of order. But he loved Sarah. Victor grabbing her like that, him ever having his hands on Sarah, over her, his *cock* in her, for fuck's sake. His large, ugly, sweaty cock that he held languidly as he pished next to Gavin in the North Stand toilets, expelling the cloudy, stagnant pill-filled lager urine into the latrine, his face twisted with a drunken belligerence that announced to the world that he was off on one for the weekend. It was too much, the idea of their cocks being in the same place, in Sarah's beautiful, beautiful cunt, no not cunt, he thought, that was a horrible word to use for her wonderful fanny. God, he wanted to kill this fucker Victor, just obliterate every fucking trace of him from this planet . . .

Sarah wanted the dentist's. She wanted it now. She was off down the road. Gavin and Victor started off after her at the same time. The three of them stumbled

. . . .

down the street in a confused and tense silence and ended up walking into the surgery together.

—Hello ... the dentist, Mr Ormiston said. — Are you all together? He was a tall, thin man, with a red face and a shock of white, wavy hair. He had large blue eyes which were magnified under his specs, giving him a crazed look.

—I'm wi her, Gavin said.

—*Ah'm* wi her! Victor snapped.

—Well, if you could wait here. Come through, my dear, Mr Ormiston said benignly, his toothy smile expanding as he ushered Sarah into his consulting room.

Gavin and Victor were left in the waiting room.

They sat in silence for a while, which Gavin broke, — Listen man, sorry aboot aw that. We werenae seein each other behind yir back. We jist went hame the gither last night.

—Did ye fuck her? Victor said in a low, ugly voice. The side of his jaw was swelling up. He was rummaging around in the pool of his own misery, testing its depths, seeing how far out he was from the edge.

—That's fuck all tae dae wi you, Gavin replied, feeling his anger rising again.

—She's ma fuckin bird!

Gavin pointed at him, — Look mate, ah ken yir upset, bit she's no your fuckin bird. She's goat a mind ay her ain n she's finished wi ye. Youse are finished, ye understand that? That's how she wis wi me last night, cause youse are finished!

Victor's face twisted into a leery smile. He looked at Gavin in a different way, like Gavin was the sad case, — Ye dinnae git it dae ye mate?

—Naw, you dinnae git it, Gavin retorted, but he could feel his confidence waning. He tried to work out why he was feeling fearful of Victor, who had backed

....

down after he had struck just one blow. It was because,
Gavin knew, he could never sustain violence. It came
to him in a reactive way, an instinctive blow, but he
lacked the stamina for a real battle. It was a good
thing Victor had backed down. Gavin couldn't bear the
thought of winners and losers, but with everyone in
the gutter, everyone debased. Violence, the warped
sibling of economics.

Victor shook his head. He felt his pain. He'd get
Mr Gavin fuckin Lover-Boy Temperley later, but the
violence of his old pal had shocked him. It had seemed
so out of character. With Sarah, that was out of
character. Gav was okay, he was sound. There was a
lot of talk about him grassing up cunts to his work at
the dole, but he could never believe that of Gav, even if
these DoE cunts put him in that position. A resignation
issue, it would be. Surely. But swing for him like that,
that wisnae Gav. Anyway, Victor rationalised, it had
been better to let Sarah see him get hurt, the sympathy
vote, he could tell it had put a bit of doubt in her.
Gavin could be taken out in other ways. — This has
happened before Gav. She's been wi other guys. But
she ey comes back tae me. Ah'm no sayin it doesnae . . .
Victor's voice rose and his fist smashed the table,
— GIT OAN MA FUCKIN TITS . . . cause it does.
It hurts cause it's ma woman.

Gavin felt deflated. He went to speak, but stopped,
knowing that his voice would come out biscuit-ersed,
that the uncertainty would be threaded right through it.

Victor continued, — She went wi Billy Stevenson the
last time. The time before that it wis Paul Younger . . .
he spat the names out like poison and Gavin shook
under them as though they were thunderbolts. He
didn't like Billy Stevenson, a smart, arrogant cunt.
Him with Sarah, it was a horrific thought. Victor's
cheesy spunk-and-lager-urinating cock inside Sarah

....

now seemed quite a pleasant consideration. Paul Younger was okay, but so fuckin anodyne. How could a woman like Sarah go with a nobody like that? Paul fuckin Younger! Victor couldn't have mentioned two more hurtful names if he'd tried.

—Billy Stevenson? Gavin repeated, hoping that he'd somehow heard wrongly.

—She did it tae git at me, for when ah went wi Lizzie Mcintosh.

So Victor had shagged Lizzie Mcintosh as well. He liked Lizzie. He knew that she punted around a bit. It was a hardly a surprise that Victor and her had got it together. That was strange. Before he had never thought of Victor and him having had their cocks in the same place. Now they had shagged not one, but at least two of the same women. He started to think about other girls he had been with that Victor might know. Edinburgh. What a fuckin place. Everybody had shagged everybody else. No wonder AIDS spread so quickly. They blamed it on the skag, but the shagging was as much to blame. It had to be. The myth that junkies didn't have a sex life. Plenty of birds wasting away in the hospice whose only injection has been the meat one could testify otherwise. He thought of Tommy; Gavin's paranoia after shagging Lizzie last year. He couldn't ask her though. Not about her and Tommy. He knew they had split up prior to Tommy getting into the junk, but he had to take the test. The demons came in the night. They always came.

—It meant fuck all man, it wis jist a ride, eh. Ye ken what it's like when yir eckied up, Victor continued. Gavin found himself nodding, stopping when it seemed too self-incriminating. Victor didn't miss the opportunity. — That wid be what it wis like wi you n her, eh?

—Naw it wisnae! It fuckin well wisnae, right!

....

163

—Well that's the wey ye'd best remember it mate, cause that's it finished.

—Naw, you n her's fuckin finished, that's what's fuckin well finished Vic. This isnae the same as her shagging some twat like Billy Stevenson or some arsehole like Younger . . . she'd jist be a ride tae they cunts, this is somebody who cares aboot her, right!

—Naw it's no fuckin right! Find yir ain fuckin bird tae care aboot! Sarah's mine! Ah love her!

—*Ah* fuckin love her!

—Yuv only kent her fir five fuckin minutes! Three fuckin *years*! Victor thrashed his chest with his fist, — Three fuckin years!

Ormiston the dentist came running through. — Please! Keep the noise down or go away! I'm having to extract two wisdom teeth here.

Gavin stiffly raised his hand to silence the dentist, then stood up over Victor, — It's her n me now ya cunt! Right! Git used tae it, cause that's the fuckin wey it is!

Victor stood up. Gavin moved back and Victor punched the air in front of him, — IS IT FUCK!

—Right! Out of here! I'm going to call the police, Mr Ormiston shouted. — Out! Now! You can wait outside! She'll be out in just over an hour! Just get the hell out of my surgery! I'm trying to extract two wisdom teeth . . . The dentist's voice disintegrated into a woeful, bewildered plea.

Victor and Gavin reluctantly shuffled outside. They stood apart from each other then Gavin sat on the steps, while Victor continued leaning against the wrought-iron railings of the New Town building.

They stared at one another for a minute, then looked away. Gavin felt himself chuckling lightly, his trickle of laughter soon becoming an uncontrollable cascade. Victor started to join in. — What are we fuckin well laughing at here? he asked, shaking his head.

. . . .

—This is mad, man . . . totally fuckin mad.

—Aye . . . lit's git a drink over there. Victor pointed to a basement pub on the corner.

They went in and Gavin bought two pints of lager. He thought he'd better pay, feeling guilty as he did about Victor's chin. Besides, Victor wasn't working, as far as he knew, though he hadn't signed on at the Leith office.

They sat in the corner, slightly apart.

Victor stared hard at his bubbling pint of lager. — Tae me, he said without looking up, — ah dinnae see how ye kin say that ye love her. He raised his head in a plea and met Gavin's eyes. — Ye wir E'd up man.

—This wis the next day though.

—It's still in yir system.

—No that long. We didnae . . . we didnae dae anything that night . . . ah mean, ah cannae make love when ah'm E'd up, ah mean ah kin make love but no git it up, if ye ken what ah mean . . . Gavin stopped, seeing Victor's face contort in rage.

—Still dinnae believe ye love her, he exhaled, gripping the table, his knuckles whitening.

Gavin shrugged, then suddenly looked inspired. — Look man, they say that Ecstasy's like a truth drug. They gie it tae couples in therapy n that . . .

—So?

—So ah *do* fuckin well love her. Ah'll prove it. Gavin pulled a small plastic bag out of the watch pocket in his jeans, tentatively extracted then swallowed a pill, washing it down with a mouthful of lager. He grimaced, then said, — It's you that doesnae love her, it's jist a habit wi you n ye cannae lit go. Feart ay rejection. That's aw it is Vic, fuckin male ego. You take one ay they pills n then tell ays ye love her when it kicks in.

Victor looked doubtfully at him, — Ah've no goat the hireys man . . .

—Fuck the hireys, this is important, this is oan me! Feeling inflated and virtuous, Gavin dug into his pocket for another pill.

—C'moan then, Victor held out his hand and took the pill from Gavin, which he quickly necked.

The pub was deserted, except for an old guy who was drinking a pint and reading a newspaper, looking a model of Sunday contentment.

Gavin went up to feed the jukebox. It was switched off. A tape with easy-listening music was playing. It was Simply Red's Greatest Hits. — It's a tape, eh, he said to Victor, who gave an uncomfortable scowl, before spinning in his seat and springing up to the bar. — What's the story wi the jukey? he asked the youngish woman behind the bar, who was washing glasses.

—Broken, she said.

Victor felt in the pocket of his bomber jacket for a tape. It was the Metalheadz Platinum Breaks. — Goan stick this oan fir ays.

—What is it? the barmaid asked.

—Bass n drum but eh.

The woman looked over in some trepidation at the old guy reading his paper, but succumbed and put the tape in the deck.

Twenty minutes later Victor and Gavin were cunted and shaking their stuff around on the floor of the deserted pub. The old guy with the pint looked up at them. Victor gave him the thumbs up and he looked away. The music was leaking into them from all sides. — J. Majik. Wait till ye hear this cunt, Victor shouted at Gavin.

After a bop, they sat down to vibe out and chat.

—Whoa man, these are fuckin strong pills, better than that shite ah hud last night, Victor acknowledged.

—Aw aye, thir something else.

—Listen mate, this isnae aboot you n me, ye ken that, eh, Victor was at some pains to express. After all, it was him and Gav.

—Tell ye what Victor, n ah'm bein honest here, ah respect ye man. Always huv, n aye, ah love ye. Yir a mate. Ah ken we're eywis in company, like say Tommy when he was here likes, Keasbo, Nelly, Spud n aw that, bit that's jist the wey it goes. Ah love ye man, Gavin hugged Victor hard and his friend reciprocated.

—Ah like you n aw Gav man, ye ken that . . . if the truth be telt yir one ay the soundest cunts ah ken. Naebody's ever goat a bad word tae say against ye man.

—Tell ye what though man, Billy Stevenson . . . that fuckin shocked me man . . .

—It cut ays up . . . it really cut ays up. Ah'd rather she went n screwed some fuckin jakey than that cunt.

—Me n aw. Ah nivir could stick that wanker.

—That's his wey though but, wait for a bird tae be feelin a bit vulnerable, a bit low, then steam in wi the smarm . . .

—Bit ah'm no like that, Gavin said, — it wisnae how it wis wi her n me. Ah widnae huv moved in if ah didnae think that youse wir history Vic. Ah'd nivir move in oan a mate's bird. Ah mean, ah didnae even think ay her at aw until last night up Tribal man. Believe it man, ah'm fuckin tellin ye. Oan ma Ma's life.

—Ah believe ye man, it's jist hard tae take, eftir three years . . .

—Bit listen mate, are ye sure thir's love left? Hus it no jist gone sour? Mibbee yir jist haudin oan, for whatever reason, mibbee ye ken yirsel deep down inside . . . ah mean, wi me n Lynda man . . . ah huv tae be honest . . . it wis like . . . it wis gone man, it wis gone, n ah wis jist hudin oan. Ah dinnae ken what fir, bit ah wis.

. . . .

Victor thought for a bit. He kept a hold of Gavin, it seemed important to do so. The pain in his jaw was now a delicious throb. He had his arm around Gavin's shoulder and the throb in his jaw seemed to pulse with the afterglow of some kind of deep communion. Maybe it was possible, maybe it was over with him and Sarah. They'd been having some terrible rows. But that was the way they were then. Now though, there was a tension and distrust between them, which, since both their infidelities had been exposed, now seemed more than just a malaise they could get out of. Maybe he had to let go, and move on.

Photek rattled around them. — Some fuckin tape eh, Gavin acknowledged.

—Metalheidz man, the fuckin best. Thuv no seen drum n bass here in Scotland man, no real bass n drum.

Gavin knew that Victor headed down to London at least once a month for the Sunday Metalheadz sessions in the Blue Note. He hadn't been able to get the vibe before, being more of a garage and soul man, but now it was obvious. This was film music. Their film. Two friends, two comrades, two Hibernian urban warriors in a battle for the heart of the beautiful woman both loved. This was the soundtrack of that horrible, beautiful movie. Life. It was sick, gorgeous nonsense.

— Listen mate, whatever happens between us n Sarah, ah want us tae stey mates. Ah want tae go doon tae London wi ye tae one ay these Metalheidz dos.

—Cool, Victor squeezed Gavin tightly.

Gavin kissed Victor on the jaw. — Sorry man, sorry ah hit ye Vic.

—Goat tae admit Gav, it wis a cracker. The first time ah've ever seen ye gub some cunt. Eywis thought ay ye as a gentle giant. Spud said ye wir a tidy cunt, at the school n that, bit that's Spud but eh. Great cunt, bit ye take whit eh sais wi a pinch ay salt. Ah wis a bit

....

shocked man, to be honest. Fuckin Gav, man, bang! Victor rubbed his jaw. — Tell ye what though Gav, it feels fuckin nice now, the throb n aw that.

—That's good. Gled it's like . . . positive, ken what ah'm sayin. Gled ah've done something positive fir ye man. Ah mean, that's aw ah want tae dae in life man, spread a positive vibe. That's ma fuckin sole ambition. N what dae ah dae? Ah go n hurt a mate. That's no me Vic, ye ken it's no me, Gavin shook his head and tears welled up in his eyes.

—Ah ken that Gav. Listen Gav . . . love man, that's the fuckin thing, Victor extended his hand and Gavin shook it, then held it and opened it, letting his index finger trace the long, deep lifeline on Victor's palm. — Lit's see what she wants tae dae, let's let love decide, Victor urged.

Gavin looked into Victor's clear, wide pupils. His soul was pure, there was no duplicity about Vic. — Lit's dae it, he whispered, then embraced Victor again.

—Right, said Victor, smile beaming broadly.

—Tae the Victor the spoils, Gavin said grandly, then laughed, — Tae the Gavin the spoils ah mean! Naw . . . may the best cunt win!

They clicked their glasses together.

Dr Ormiston had Sarah on the chair. He was looking down at her as she stared up at the ceiling, looking fretful. She was a fetching girl all right, her long legs in that short skirt, her hands clasped across what looked like a very nice chest, and that chestnut hair swept back from her face cascading out across the headrest of his chair. He had to concede, he could see what all the hoo-ha was about with those two young bucks. He felt a flutter in his chest, as her scent and perfume filled his nostrils. There was nothing like the succulent flesh of a young female, he thought, licking his lips. — Open wider, he gasped, as his pulse skipped a beat and his cock stiffened.

There was no drill, she was thinking, thank fuck there was no drill. But there was the knife, and the sound it made, picking, prodding, rending and sawing at her numbed flesh. She couldn't feel the damage, but she could hear it.

A beautiful mouth. It was always the first thing Ormiston noticed in a woman. Full lips, strong, white teeth. There was a bit of neglect inside here however. A shameful waste. A woman like this should floss.

Sarah looked at the dentist's intense electric blue eyes, the white hairs on his eyebrows which joined in the middle. It seemed that he was looking right into her, sharing a strange kind of intimacy with her that no man had ever had. She saw her mouth in his mirror. But not the wound. She couldn't look at the wound. Nor the pliers, especially not the pliers. Something hard was digging into her thigh. It might have been a rest on the chair. The man's breathing was becoming irregular, but Ormiston was her saviour. This would be the man who would liberate her from the sickening, all-pervading pain. This man, with his education, his skill and, yes, compassion, for a man capable of success in the field of dentistry could surely have chosen a more lucrative sphere. How much did they get paid? This man would sweep aside the misery and everything would be as it was. Victor would do nothing, Gavin could do nothing, but this man, he would take away the pain.

—It's got to come out now, he yanked and twisted, ripping into her numbed flesh around the back of her gums. It was a shame to lose those wisdom teeth, and Ormiston always mourned what he gloomily referred to as the death of a tooth, but in this case, there was no alternative. This girl had simply had too many teeth

....

170

for her head. The extraction of both bottom wisdom teeth was essential. He leaned into her and let his free hand rest on her hip. She squirmed a little and he apologised, — Sorry, I just need to get leverage . . .

The suction tube removed the saliva from her mouth. He moved his free hand up and pulled it languidly around inside her, poking it into every cavity, sucking all her sweet, sweet juices, oh God her gorgeous mouth . . . he couldn't help but imagine his tongue in that mouth, the clean, sharp probing tongue of a man who used all the proven-to-be-effective rather than gimmicky dental products on the market, and he let his hand move down and why was she wearing that skirt, he could feel her naked thigh against his hand the hairs on the back of it bristling and him now imagining it going between her legs and his fingers inside her wee cotton briefs and her hungry dripping pussy eating them and one more wrench and her tooth came free in his pliers as he ejaculated into his pants. — That was a hard one, he gasped, as his cock spurted spasmodically in his trousers. He turned away as the spunk pumped into his flannels and his prick throbbed rawly. — Ah . . . ah . . . a satisfactory extraction . . . he wheezed, trying to compose himself.

Sarah felt uncomfortable and went to mumble something, but he told her to keep quiet. He worked away at the second tooth and extracted it more easily than the first one.

He took great care cleaning and packing her wounds. Her mouth was numb as she spat out the wash, but Sarah felt a tremendous relief.

—I thought I'd better get them both out as you'd only have to go through the same rigmarole again shortly, Ormiston explained.

—Thanks, Sarah said.

—No, the pleasure was all mine . . . I mean, you have

beautiful teeth, and you really should floss them. Now that the wisdom teeth are out, they shouldn't be so tightly packed together. There's no excuse now! Get that floss working!

—Aye, I will, she said.

—Lovely teeth, Ormiston shuddered. — No wonder you have those young men fighting over you!

Sarah blushed, and felt bad for blushing. It was just the man's way however. He wasn't being creepy, he was a professional, it was just another mouth to him.

Ormiston *was* a professional man, and as such not wont to letting aesthetic considerations take precedence over finance, and he composed himself sufficiently to charge Sarah seventy pounds, for which she had to write out a cheque.

—I'd like to see you again in a fortnight's time, Ormiston smiled. —Unfortunately, because it's an emergency call-out, we don't have a duty receptionist. But if you give me a note of your address and phone number, I'll arrange for an appointment to be made for you.

—Thanks, Sarah said. Even the loss of seventy quid couldn't take away the sense of relief. Sorry to get you out on a Sunday, I hope I didn't spoil your day.

—Not at all, my dear, not at all. Ormiston smiled. He watched her depart, and his face sank into a frown as he contemplated the mind-numbing tedium of a family Sunday at Ravelston Dykes. — Bugger it, he hissed softly, then went to the toilet to clean himself up.

Sarah heard her name being called. She looked across the road, where Victor and Gavin were standing, outside the pub. She moved towards them. They were both regarding her brightly, but seemed at peace with each other.

—How did it go? Gavin asked. — Are ye okay?

....

172

—Much better, just a bit numb. They took ma wisdom teeth oot.

—Come in n sit doon, Victor implored.

As Sarah sat down Gavin gave her a full embrace. It felt a bit strange. For Gavin it was great to hold her and to smell her hair and perfume and feel her warmth. Then he saw Victor out of the corner of his eye and felt bad that he was excluded. He pulled Victor towards them and they had a group hug with Sarah feeling awkward and self-conscious in the middle. — Sarah . . . Victor . . . Sarah . . . Victor . . . Gavin moaned, kissing their faces alternately.

She looked out across the pub at the old guy with the pint and smiled in benign embarrassment. He tetchily looked away. Two younger guys came in and looked, then shrugged and smiled.

—Sarah . . . Sarah . . . Sarah . . . Victor started a sad mantra, — aw doll ah'm really sorry. Ah'm a prick, a total fuckin prick.

Sarah considered that it was hard to dispute this contention.

—Ah love ye Sarah. Ah'm in love wi ye, Gavin was mumbling in her other ear.

For a few very brief moments it seemed to her that it was like sticking a load of After Eight mints into your mouth: you were lulled by the sudden sweetness of it, until the sickness and self-loathing overwhelmed you. — Fuckin let go ay me! She snapped, pulling away and looking at Victor's raised hands and Gavin's forlorn, sad eyes. — What yis fuckin like! Yis are E'd up!

—Ah love ye Sarah, ah mean it, Gavin said.

—Ah love ye, but ah think it isnae workin oot. Ah want ye tae be happy n if this big cunt's makin ye mair happy than ah could, well, that's the wey it is. Ah want tae ken though, what's the story doll?

. . . .

173

The story was that these things were invading her space, like huge, creepy twisting plants wrapping around her as her comedown kicked in and her nerve ends, twisted and raw, rebelled against their insinuation. They didn't get it; it was like she didn't exist in her own right, like she was a thing to be fought over. Territory. Land. Possession. That was Victor. That was him. When they made up, after she went with that guy from Yip Yap, the way he had fucked her; hard, rampantly, in every orifice, as if to reclaim territory lost, devoid of tenderness and sensuality. She'd lain there on the floor, trying to hide tears she knew he'd seen but hadn't acknowledged. She felt like she'd been beaten, punished, used; like he'd tried to fuck anything the other guy may have left in her out of her. And that was just the sex. No way was Sarah going to be on the receiving end of Victor's sexual and psychological scorched-earth policy again. Him and Gavin together. Colluding now. At first conflict over territory, but now those fraternal brothers realise that it cannot be resolved by military means. Let's get round the table and thrash this out.

It was not (a) leaves Victor and falls in love with Gavin and lives happily ever after, or (b) fucks Gavin but realises error of ways and goes back to Victor and lives happily ever after. It was (c) left Victor, fucked Gavin. Past tense in both cases. It's over, you silly wee laddies, well fuckin over you sad, self-mythologising egotistical ratbags.

She writhed free from them, stood up and shook her head. This was too much. She looked at Victor, — You're a prick, you're right enough there. Git oot ma fuckin face, how many times dae ah have tae tell ye, it's over! N you, she fumed to Gavin whose eyes had gone even more baleful, — we had a fuckin shag, that's aw! If it wis any mair tae you, tell *me* aboot it, no him,

....

n tell ays when yir no fill ay chemicals. Now fuck off n leave ays alaine, the pair ay yis! She stood up and moved towards the exit of the pub.

—Ah'll gie ye a bell the night . . . Gavin said, hearing his voice crack like a light bulb and the 'night' part become incomprehensible.

—Jist fuck off! she fumed and sneered, and left.

—Well, said Gavin turning to Victor with a hint of self-satisfaction, — there it is. You're bombed oot fir good, bit ah'm still in there. Ah just see her when ah'm straight n pit her in the picture.

Victor shook his head, — Ye dinnae ken Sarah but eh. That's no what ah goat fae it at aw.

They argued for a while, punctuating their points with friendly squeezes on each other's wrists to maintain their communion.

A man entered the pub at this point, a man whom both recognised. It was the dentist, Mr Ormiston. He bought a half-pint of heavy and sat at a table close to them reading *Scotland on Sunday*. He noticed them out of the corner of his eye. Gavin grinned and Victor raised his pint glass. Ormiston gave a weary smile back. It was the two young bucks. Where was the girl?

—Sorry aboot the Edinburgh mate, Victor said, — Bet ye wir well fuckin zorba'd at that, eh.

—Pardon? Ormiston looked puzzled.

—Didnae mean tae involve you in aw that nonsense in yir surgery. Sorted her oot but mate, eh?

—Oh yes. Pretty nasty routine extractions. Wisdom teeth can be tricky, but all in a day's work.

Victor moved closer to Ormiston. — Some joab you've goat but mate, eh. Ah couldnae dae that. Lookin in cunts' mooths aw day. He turned to Gavin. — Widnae be me!

Gavin looked thoughtfully at the dentist. — They

....

175

tell ays that ye need as much trainin tae be a dentist as ye dae tae be a doaktir. Is that right mate?

—Well, as a matter of fact it is . . . Ormiston began, in the somewhat self-justifying air of a man who regards his profession as crassly misunderstood by the lay-person.

—Shite! Victor interrupted, — Youse kin git the fuck oot ay here, the pair ay yis! A dentist you've goat jist the mooth tae deal wi, whereas doaktirs, these cunts've goat the whole boady! Yir no tryin tae tell ays that a dentist needs the same amount ay trainin as a doaktir!

—Naw, bit it's no the same thing Vic. By the same fuckin logic, that means that a vet wid need mair trainin than a doaktir, because they've goat tae learn no jist aboot humans bit aboot cats n dugs, n rabbits, n cows . . . the physiology ay aw they different animals.

—Ah nivir sais that, Victor insisted, wagging his finger at Gavin.

—Ah'm jist sayin thit it's the same fuckin principles involved here, that's aw ah'm sayin. Tae tend tae a whole creature needs mair trainin than tae tend tae one part ay a creature. That's what yir sayin, aye?

—Aye, right, Victor conceded. Ormiston tried to get back to his paper.

—So by the same logic, tendin tae different crea-tures'll mean mair trainin than tendin tae the jist one creature. Right?

—Uh-uh-uh-uh-uh . . . Victor halted him. — It does-nae follow. This is human society we're talkin aboot here. Right?

—So?

—So it isnae fuckin cat society or dug society . . .

—Wait the now . . . Gavin nodded. — What you're sayin is thit in oor society humans are the maist valued species, so the level ay investment in the trainin ay people tae tend humans . . .

—... will exceed the level ay investment in the trainin gied tae people tae tend tae animals. Hus tae be the wey Gav. Victor turned to Ormiston. — Is that no right but mate?

—Yes, I suppose that's a point, the dental surgeon said distractedly.

Gavin was thinking about this. There was something that was jarring him. The way people treated animals was out of order. And him too, he hadn't even fed the cat. Out for two days off on one, and he'd forgotten about a promise that he'd made to his ma, that he'd go round to hers and feed the cat. She was away up to Inverness to her sister's. She was mad about that cat. She even called it Gavin sometimes by mistake, which hurt him more than he let on. He felt a surge of guilt. — Vic, ah've goat tae nash. You've jist reminded ays, ah said ah'd go roond ma Ma's n feed the cat. Ah'm fuckin oot ay order here. The last thing she made ays promise. He stood up and Victor did too. They had another hug. — Nae hard feelins mate?

—Naw man ... ah jist hope she comes back tae ays, Victor said wearily.

—Well mate, ye ken ma feelins oan that yin ... Gavin nodded.

—Aye ... take care Gav. We're at hame next Setirday. Aberdeen, eh, the cup.

—Aye. Which means season effectively over in January unless ye count a possible relegation battle.

—It's a tough joab mate, bit some cunt's goat tae dae it. See ye doon the Four-in-Hand.

—Right.

Gavin turned and left the pub. He walked up the hill at Hanover Street, or Hangover Street, as they called it. The effects of the MDMA were running down in him and a shiver coursed through his body, although it wasn't cold. He pulled a flyer for a club night out of his pocket. Written on it was the name SARAH and a seven-digit phone number. He should just be able to phone that number. It was love, it was. It shouldn't need an ideal place or an ideal time to be expressed. It should just happen.

There was a phone box. There was an Asian woman in it. He wanted to finish that call. More than anything. Then he became aware of his heart, thrashing in his chest. He couldn't speak to her like this, he'd fuck it up again. He wanted the woman to stay on the phone for ever. Then she put the receiver down on the cradle. Gavin turned away and walked down the road. Now wasn't the time. Now was the time to get to his mother's and feed Sparky the cat.

Acid Burns

DAVID TOOP

The way it started out, Ricky was still cutting neat little two-inch slits in the bottom seam of his jeans, fit them nicely over gleaming slip-ons, show a flash of white sock, get a bit of fraying happening at pavement level. Discreet, nothing flash, nothing hippie. Just a bit of detail for the old fast footwork. He even tried bleach for the white lightning effect. Felt a right woofter after the chemistry turned him into a walking burns victim. This particular experiment in dermatology finished up with one pair red legs and one pair arse-out jeans the colour of semi-skimmed, equalling the price of at least three import albums and a 12 from City Sounds, equalling a total, utter piss-off for one entire rotation of the sun. Or is it the earth? Twenty-four hours, anyway, at least.

Ricky's younger brother, Lee, was already shifting this and moving that, suited double-breastedly onwards and upwards, blond highlights, driving a proper car and getting his pipes lagged on a regular basis. Oblivious to the bigger picture, Ricky focused his all on the mafia, the jocks who ruled. They'd held off disco, fuckin' electro, rap and all the shite black America could throw across the Atlantic. The whole lot of them, Ricky especially, not that he was afforded access to the inner sanctum as yet but wait and see, knew in their deepest hearts, guarded by wallets stuffed with big ones, that the likes of George Duke and Stanley Clarke held the secrets of the universe in their wiggly fingers. Course they were black, but no way could any poxy computer play real music like that. Jazz, you know what I mean?

Socially speaking, Ricky's finest moment up until the present tense was Maze, 'Joy and Pain', Wembley Arena. Pissed, he and Dawn sang it all the way home, then did their own joy and pain on the shagpile till Ricky complained he'd have to go out to 7–11 and buy some more spunk. Dawn started shagging Lee on the shagpile two weeks later. Pissed again, Ricky had to administer some bruise make-up to Dawn's tearful face, prior to the final touching good-byes and fare-thee-wells. Lee got off lightly, Ricky just tossing all his crap Spandau Ballet albums into the dirt where they belonged. Can't spank your own flesh and blood, can you? Not for a cunt like Dawn, anyway, good fucking riddance.

So Ricky's working his way up to mafia membership, maybe end up organising weekenders for shaggers and piss-artists at some freezing poxy Pontins by the Arctic Sea, doing some A&R, meeting Fatback backstage at Hammersmith, even shaking hands with Chris Hill or Robbie Vincent. At the end of this particular tunnel he sees a Roller, him ensconced within and champagned to the eyeballs just like that fat bastard DJ who died from being fat. The one who made a dog's turd of a record by shouting 'Whoa-oh, whoa-oh' over the top of somebody else's tune.

In the interim, doubtless brief though dragging on a bit as of late, Ricky's running a night up Tottenham High Road, doing soul and jazz-funk for the ethnic population and their natural born enemies, the Blond Wedge Mr Byrite tribes of Wood Green, Bounds Green and other greenish outlands. Come the third or fourth pint of foreign lager, studying distant crumpet and its sweating masters in the Jolly Butcher's, deep in the

....

outer mediocrity of Enfield, Ricky's safety zone that is, the old refrain starts.

'Me, I'm not a fucking racist,' says Ricky to John, who is a roofer of sufficient distinction to be able to buy the lion's share of rounds for at least three sessions out of every four. 'First record I ever bought was black music. I don't buy white music. Never have. Fucking rock music, lotta noise and words about fuck all that makes any sense. If I was on that Radio One I'd play fusion, twenty-four hours a day. Get Bob James on Top of the Cuntish Pops. Yeah, I know Bob James is white but it's black music, innit? Look at Tony Blackburn, all right he's a wanker, you've got to laugh, all that hot throbbing twelve-inch bollocks, but he plays good music, always did. That red jacket's crap though.'

None the less, Ricky sees himself as Speke, searching out the source of the Nile. When he has found it, bathed his feet, studied his handsome reflection, shagged the native bearers, feasted on zebra and pissed in the tropical waters, he will turn back for the Geographical Society in civilised Piccadilly, there to bask in wealth and glory. Time will deliver in backdated fruitfulness, despite the lateness of the hour.

The haircut changes it all. Like something out the Bible. Hair's losing its shape, roots giving the game away, bald patch developing fast, go for a quick refit. To be utterly truthful, the haircut is symptomatic. Tucked away at some considerable distance behind Mr Cocky's who-gives-a-toss is Ricky's underground cavern of despair, this being a place where the truth of it all resides in squalor and stink. For Ricky knows, in his heart, that he's fucked, nowhere to go, no earthly use to the planet, not fit for human consumption. Getting too old to pull, musical tastes lately regarded as sharing a time zone with Glenn Miller, nurtured style caught in sideways glance on off-licence security

....

monitors and stirring up chilly blasts of panic. The applicable phrase is ready to hand, if only because Ricky has used it as a weapon against others. Now the wounds are self-inflicted. Out of touch.

Then *Boom*, the second coming, pillar of salt, struck down by blinding light, balls cut off and rolling across the floor. Waiting his turn, Ricky sits with a marked absence of relaxation, anxious about the future, bored due to a permanent dose of imagination deficiency syndrome. Stillness and reflection, for Ricky, are a foreign country, yet he can feel the truth stirring in its lair. Acting on primal instinct, he decides to read the *Sun*, which is an activity unknown to him save for studying the third page and fantasising a relationship between tit volume and his erect penis. For some unknown reason, perhaps a miracle, he reads the front page and discovers a new phrase.

Acid House.

Now house music, for Ricky, though he is not fully comprehensive on the issue, shares a rung on the evolutionary ladder with Jethro Tull and Mantovani. Not only does it appear to be disco for homos and drug addicts. Worse, terminally, it is made by machines. He has never, in his born days, heard a decent keyboard solo in a house music record. When his hero, Herbie Hancock, started recording that electro shit he had gagged until his eyes watered. House music, by comparison, is like being trussed up in electrified razor wire and sodomised by a road drill.

Independently, his eyes roam different parts of the story. The slender gist, if he followed, is some crap about parties and drugs. Drugs of the sort Ricky abhors and fears. Drugs that drag the engine of time to a standstill between stations. Drugs that transformed Mum's carpet into a nest of Persian serpents and jewel-encrusted parasites. Drugs that make Roy Ayers sound

....

like the Grateful Dead. Drugs and parties. Parties and acid house, whatever the frigging animal that is when it answers the doorbell.

Ricky's post-wedge trim passes in a dream. The sad fact of the matter sits and gazes back at him from the mirror. This is, in name and substance, himself, newly shorn yet intractably a loser to rank alongside every one of his peers. For his jazz-funk mission in Tottenham, he surmises, there is little more than a malarial future.

There are times in the life of a man when habit falls away with every snip of the barber's scissors. Ricky takes himself to the Favourite Restaurant, eats two fried eggs, sausage, chips, beans, brown sauce, salt, bread and butter, tea with three sugars, and changes course, doggedly, wave by wave, swallow by swallow, pointing his prow towards the eye of the storm. Later that fateful day, he visits his old mum, a duty that entails a rail excursion into the northbound corridor, passing Edmonton, Bruce Grove, Turkey Street, cementscapes, dust-obscured posters for events that have been and gone, post-war terraces, overloaded buses crawling through avenues of emission-encrusted real-hair wig shops, kebab take-outs, deep-pan pizza and video clubs into regions where a breaker's yard is a feature of distinction, a beauty spot almost, places where dogs fight to the bloody death in squalid sheds, British Movement enclaves conduct their seances in dirty little maisonettes and, shrouded by night, fishermen sit in monkish nocturnal vigil, cut adrift from job, wife, kids, the forces of order.

'You're like your father, Richard,' says old Mum, lighting a fag. 'Always schemes but nothing on the table. When he died, all we had was bills. Nothing ever came to nothing.'

Fortified by the chill wind of destiny, Richard, as he

....

has become for the evening, stares at the television screen, *Celebrity Squares* it seems, and resolves to do better.

Ricky is haunted by a recurrent fantasy. In a rush of blood, it comes to him again that night, foetal and restive in the spare room at old Mum's. The focus of this rare act of imagination is random, being any one of the more attractive black women who attend Cracker's, stripped to underwear clichés, down on elbows and knees, Ricky inserting his somewhat average penis with the studied nonchalance of a man filling up the motor with five star. Fantasy being more tangible than the real thing right now, he has to wank and feels like a small boy again, old Mum sleeping on the other side of the flower-papered wall but no doubt sensing at some deep maternal level the mechanical labours of her son, the impotent schemer.

Climax-effective the fantasy might be, yet Ricky cannot bring himself to trust a black person. Despite a lot of verbal noise, nervous laughter and high fives, the crabwise heft and creak of his body language betray him. A mortal terror clings to the internal walls of his guts and will not be shaken loose even by abstruse discussion of the Dexter Wansell discography. A tight clutch of young Asians attend his night at Cracker's but he scarcely notes their presence. How can they be players in the game of life? How can anybody who eats liquid fire and listens to that Ravi Shankar shit ever join him on the mountaintop, breathing the high thin air of jazz fusion? Mind you, Ricky likes a curry now and then.

This fear and contempt is part of the urban texture. Ricky's most concentrated hatred is held on the back burner, however, maintained at a steady temperature for application against white people who claim familiarity with black music. The fact that this category is applicable to himself and most of his friends is an anomaly that fails to compute. No white person who listens to black music can be as serious as he and his circle, so they must be listening for the sake of mere fashion, or because they have graduated from Abba and David Bowie to the Truth.

When it comes to the big decision, such a quarter-pounder of confusion can only enrich Ricky's fervour. For once in his life, he is convinced through desperate inspiration rather than prejudice. Some research is in order. Ricky splashes out on a copy of *Echoes*. He reads more headlines in the *Sun*. Standing in his local newsagents, he ignores abuse from behind the counter and crawls through a page of the *NME*. Back home and cradling a Brew he watches snooker, Jimmy White losing to Steve Davis, and as the balls sink into their string scrota with a steady meditational pock-pock, black after red, red after black, so Ricky assembles his fragments of knowledge into something that could be mistaken for a plan.

Jazz-Funkateers at Cracker's will become Ricky's Acciieeed Burn!! That is the long and short of it, the blind and the hopeless, the good, the bad and the ugly. Maybe three exclamation marks, but those are details for the attention of Big Frank, Waltham Abbey printer for three generations and part-time security consultant.

So change is effected. Even Ricky is moved by the verbal pitch he delivers to Gladys, ex-madam in her twilight years, now public face of the otherwise secretive Cracker's Management Team.

'I seen it all,' she says. 'White boys with long hair, white boys with shaved head. Fist fights, razor fights, glue sniffing, pills to make you quick, pills to make you slow. I seen every drug under the sun. I seen torture

....

and mayhem. Boys dressed as girls, girls dressed as boys. Girl with skirt up round her pussy, girl with skirt dragging in the dust. I seen black shoot white, poom poom, seen white hit black with pipe, squit like stepping on a snail. I seen black and white turn on Indian man and pull him limb from limb. I seen girls raped, seen blind men so drunk they have to pay a girl to help them piss. I seen famous people play here. I seen the dance bands, ska bands, blues bands, rock bands, soul bands, reggae music, disco. My husband, rest in peace, served a drink one time to that boy Jermaine Jackson. I seen the whole world at night, right here.'

Ricky waits for the punch line. 'OK,' she says. A long pause, police sirens going off somewhere in the distance, a phone ringing. 'OK, OK. We try your acid.'

Now Ricky needs some records. Better still, a DJ with his own records. Breaking the habit of a lifetime, he ventures into Soho.

With City Sounds, Ricky knows where he is. A shop for real music, run by good blokes, up for a laugh and a drink. They sell rap and house, can't avoid it, every bastard's got to make a fair crack, but you don't have to hear too much of it in the shop. What Ricky has to do now is expand his horizons.

For years he's known about Groove, heard all the rumours, sometimes went in when it was a hole-in-the-wall near Ronnie Scott's, open at night and run by an old woman who looked like she should be selling tea, sugar and Marmite. Unnerving it was. Ricky bought a Little Beaver album once and blushed when he said 'Beaver'.

Groove moved to the corner of Greek Street and Bateman, windows on two sides so every tart and pimp in Soho could follow your whereabouts. Now they do house and hip-hop. What is worse is the knowledge

....

that a few doors along is a place that sells 140 bpm hi-energy and Italian shit sung by women with big tits and plastic wigs, shop full of blokes with moustaches and short hair. Not to mention bookshops, poncey restaurants and windows dressed with rock guitars. This environment makes Ricky very nervous.

But being old-school has its perks. In the upper regions, Ricky would be one of the first to admit a certain lack, but around the chest area he stores a hefty wodge of pride and somewhere between gut and balls he keeps bottle. Only about a half pint but enough for a foray on Venus.

Groove is a tough nut to crack. First, you have to wedge in between the DJs who wrap themselves around the counter, two deep and seemingly idle for the duration. The old woman is still there, sitting down, smiling at the regulars, pulling out a 12 when business gets quick. The bloke serving doesn't really serve. He just mixes. Ricky wants to ask some questions, just casual, but the bass bins hidden under the browser racks are flapping his jeans. Casual just isn't in it; you have to blow your lungs out to get attention. Fucking ridiculous.

'Got any acid?'

Nobody takes a blind bit of notice.

'Got any acid, mate?'

Mister Groove reaches out, not looking where his hand is going, flash git, picks up a 12, slides a fader, slips it into the mix. Ricky has no idea if this is a response to his question but what he hears is about as close to torture as you can get without strapping your dick to a hot iron.

'Yeah, right,' he says. Off the deck, to Ricky's relief, and into a yellow bag, no messing. A fiver down already. Worse than the betting shop.

'Got any more? New stuff?'

'Van's in at three,' says Mister Groove.

....

Ricky studies his watch and computes embarrassment factor over the square root of torment. Twenty-five minutes, so he retreats to the browsers to browse. What strikes him with some force is this. After a lifetime of following black music in all shapes and forms, he no longer has a clue what's going on. Not a single name on any record makes so much as a faint bonging sound of recognition in his head. Utter silence. In fact, most of these people sound like they're fucking South American. On the other hand, Ricky's not such a moron that he can't deduce a few acid references here and there. 'Acid Tracks', 'Acid Over', 'I've Lost Control' and the like. Even one called 'Washing Machine', which sounds about right. He decides to cut and run, passing the covers over the counter and doing a Paul Daniels on some club flyers as he transfers more than thirty quids of dosh in exchange for vinyl.

The flyers are a bonus. Fridge on Friday and Trip's not till next week but Regine's Indy Acid is tonight, a Wednesday, so Ricky has seven hours to kill, approximately. He does this in the Odeon, Leicester Square, watching *Wall Street*, and in various pubs, all of them occupied by American tourists, Japanese tourists, Tibetan tourists for all Ricky knows, plus a potpourri of poofs, tarts and generalised wankers. By 10.00 p.m. he is quite drunk, ready to be the Gordon Gekko of clubland, ready for acid.

Regine's Indy Acid is held in a club otherwise noted for a clientele of German au pairs and Italian stallions. Heart slipping to the level of his slip-ons, Ricky watches a trickle of seventies glitter, post-Goth and Indo-hippie uniforms slip past him. Moving forward, he walks into an arm belonging to some black bloke wearing a black overcoat over black tie.

'Sorry sir, private party tonight.'

'Don't gimme that bollocks,' says Ricky.

....

Not ten minutes later he is searching for his car around Chinatown, pissed beyond recognition, sore in the cheekbone area, jeans arse-out all over again.

Flaming August begins, heralded on Tottenham High Road by the launch of Ricky's Acciieeed Burn!!! Big Frank felt confident, no extra charge, that an extra exclamation mark would push the floating voters out of their apathy.

Ricky fidgets around the door, making geometric patterns between DJ booth and toilet, then back to the door. As luck would have it, a drink in Cheshunt turned into something more productive than a headache. His old mate Steve, hearing the sad story of Ricky's allergic reaction to his acid house purchases, connects him with an electrician, who, as it goes, spins a tune or two on the Saturday night party circuit in Hertfordshire's wild and remote places. Welwyn, for instance. And Potter's Bar. Brookmans. Hatfield being the high spot.

'He plays a lot of shit for twenty-firsts, stag nights, hen nights, silver weddings, all that bollocks,' says Steve.

The electrician does well. Liberated, as he perceives it, as aspirational boys will, from a dungeon governed by Neighbours cast-offs and lesser mortals, he undergoes a personality transformation which is tempered only by the difficulty of meeting vinyl desires with pecuniary advantage.

Having smashed down every door of adversity, Ricky is crestfallen at the sight of his early-bird punters. Virgins for burning, they stroll past Big Frank without so much as a care in the world, her in white shoes, spray-on dress and matching handbag, him looking a bit Bros, blonded, 501s with lunchbox, towelling socks and questionable fashion details.

'Oh dear me,' thinks Ricky. 'Oh fucking no way, José.'

....

The cream of north London's most mental this is not.

Then two blokes in vivid shell suits. Whatever happened to dress codes? Worser and worser, Ricky tells himself.

Contemplating the future, post-apocalypse, Ricky is approached in an encouragingly shy manner by a man wearing glasses, generally looking all wrong. 'Hello, I'm a journalist,' says the bloke. 'I'm doing a newspaper story about acid house. Broadsheet, not tabloid. The doorman told me you were Ricky.'

Ricky beams. A journalist. Not an animal he has ever seen, either in zoo, wild habitat or post-mortem. As his mouth opens and shuts, sounds emerging, he wonders how he should talk.

'All right mate?' he says, breezier than he feels. 'Enjoying yourself? Drink?'

'Enjoyment's relative,' says the journalist, judging himself to be in the presence of a thick-headed chancer. 'I want to ask you a few questions about acid. I mean, there's not much of a crowd here, is there? Why put on an acid night here? More white shoes round the handbag, isn't it?'

Ricky wants to give this ponce a hard smack but the novelty of an alien visitation mutes his primal response. They drift to the bar where Ricky is obliged to order a mineral water, which is another new experience.

'Well, it's something different, yeah?' he chirps, ever the chirpy chappie. 'I give it till the end of the summer, as it goes. All over by then. We'll have some real music back by winter. All right for kids though, innit?'

Journalist smirks, jotting in his little jotter. Not the grabbiest sound bite in history but rich in potential for a class war chuckle.

'What kind of music do you really like, yourself?'

'Jazz,' says Ricky, feeling that warm seducing glow

....

190

stoked by curiosity, particularly curiosity voiced by a stranger, out of the blue. An innocent, Ricky fails to identify the professional component of the question, by far its greater part, and the sniff of an autobiographical soliloquy clouds his judgement with more devastating effect than a gallon of eight per cent lager.

'Tell me more,' the journalist invites, face open as a sunflower.

And Ricky does. And does. And completely does.

When he has nothing more to say, the jotting long since curtailed, he looks around to realise that money is being lost, here and now. On behalf of the Cracker's Management Team, Gladys will not be well pleased in any shape or form.

'All right? Get what you need?' he asks.

'Oh yes,' says the journalist. 'Plenty.'

Later that evening, Lee pokes his snotty nose in the door.

'How's it going, Rick?'

'Look at it. Fucking useless.'

'You wanna move somewhere with a bit more class. Move into town.'

Lee's shifting money around these days, so figures he has the final say on matters of class, classy and classiness. The suburbs can no longer pump his tyres.

'Yeah, well . . .' says Ricky.

In a rare fit of compassion, Lee changes the subject. His conversational tack is not a happy one.

'Guess who I saw up the Weavers?'

'Fuck knows.'

'Dawn. Well pissed. Said she fancied seeing you again. Nice tits.'

Demonstrably uncheered by nostalgia, or the reminder of Dawn's physique, Ricky makes more than the customary number of shoulder shrugs that communicated unease.

'Want a pint?'

'Nah. This place is a shithole. I only came to have a laugh.'

Ricky turns away. In the darkness of Cracker's he tunes out, melting into a foggy dream soundtracked by MFSB's 'Universal Love'. All broken angles and shadow, his father is sitting in the lounge, watching some shite on the television. Ricky sits with him, just for a moment, he tells himself. They both stare screenwards, parallel sightlines.

'Rick, your mum's talking about leaving. Or kicking me out. Says I'm worst than useless.'

Mute, Ricky wants to cry. He wants to smash a window. He wants to go back to his room. Drown in the bass. Piss off everything. Just listen to his music.

Within two weeks, acid house is blowing up. More *NME* features, first youth movement since punk and all that, more rumbling in the tabloids and anthropological fieldwork in the broadsheets, even a bit of *Top of the Pops* action in the offing. None of this hyperbole has radiated out Tottenham way. Ricky's Acciieeed Burn!!! is on low gas in the bowels of the oven and Gladys is looking more awkward by the minute. Her son, a nasty piece of work, has taken to muttering in her ear when Ricky is around. 'Rumours' by Gregory Isaacs is burning up the sounds, making the girls and the boys happy, and Gladys, ever the dutiful parent, is heeding the wisdom of her son.

'I think we going to have a lovers' reggae night back,' she says.

Ricky shivers in the summer heat.

Yet this is turning out to be the summer of love and Ricky has a little time yet to find a primrose pathway to the glowing heart pump of this love season.

Fourth night of Ricky's Acciieeed Burn!!! is looking

like an unmitigated disaster. Neck stretched like a chicken, Ricky feels the gleaming blade of Lovers' Night straining above him, poised to drop. Two hours into an increasingly desolate evening two geezers approach, one gelled and shiny, white shirt glowing like a spirit manifestation in the UV strip light, the other wearing a spotted bandanna, surfer shorts, dark round glasses and a horizontal-stripe T-shirt.

'All right matey?' says Hair Gel. 'Quiet night? Fucking right.'

'It'll pick up later,' says Ricky.

'Smile please. I think we may just be able to help you out,' says Stripey, posh drawl causing Ricky to set his mouth in that tight strip of repressed hostility common to the condescended.

'How's that?'

Hair Gel motions them into the shadows behind a booth, pulls out a clear plastic box full of gelatine bullets and colourful pills, as yet obscure and unsung though destined for celebrity. He nods in the direction of Big Frank, standing next to the luminescent Over 21s poster.

'Tell your hard nut over there we got a franchise in place. Shift a few of these, you got a better atmosphere, more punters coming in. I mean, be honest, wankers drinking Heineken, vodka tonics, rather be jigging about to Wet Wet Wet.'

'Once we're up and running,' says Stripey, 'we'll cut you in. You'll make a bundle.'

'What are they?' says Ricky, antennae twitching.

'Ecstasy mate. Other stuff, too, but that's the big one. Just make you feel all's right with the world, straight.'

'Try one,' says Stripey, smirking, lit up by the challenge. 'It'll put hairs on your chest.'

By this point in the brief history of Ricky's Acciieeed Buzz!!!, Ricky has endured one smirk too many. He

....

remembers his father, droning on about the old days, present misfortune just a temporary phase, glittering future ahead and all that. Plans and schemes and fucking fairy dust. Right now, Ricky has never felt so low. Be honest, he couldn't care less if he took a pill and it turned him into a baboon. Life in the primate world could hardly be a retrogression.

'Not weird or nothing, is it?' says Ricky.

'No mate. Ever taken speed?'

Ricky nods, a conspirator at last.

'There you go then.'

He sees the trap but what the fuck, down the neck.

The night drags one foot in front of the other and Ricky's too busy sorting out minor altercations on the dance floor to notice much in the way of metabolic change. Mr DJ has twigged that acid may not be the promised escape route out of Herts; he is unsure, he says, about next week. As for Big Frank, an air of scepticism has settled on that normally imperturbable surface. Ricky does feel a rush at one point, a tingling of nerve ends and thundering of blood which makes him assume that uncontrollable conversation about utter bollocks is imminent, but Gladys and her terrible son request an audience in the Cracker's office. The buzz is put to one side, to develop as it will.

Terrible son sitting over by the permanently cur-tained window, Gladys fixes Ricky with a stare that Kali, goddess of destruction, might be proud to possess in her armoury of scary looks.

'Ricky, we going to do the Lovers' Night,' she says. 'I can't even pay the electric with your bar takings and this acid music give me a headache.'

Expecting to be crushed by bad tidings, Ricky feels a wave of optimism tremble through his body. Nostalgic even in bliss, a Joe Sample tune dances in his head.

....

Free at last, free at last. He smiles the cheesiest smile of his life.

'I fucking hate reggae,' he offers as a token of companionability.

Terrible son glowers.

'You finish up tonight, find yourself some other place,' says Gladys in frosted tones, an experienced judge of character who's had Ricky's measure all along.

Floating back into the room, the grin still in place, Ricky spots Hair Gel and Stripey on the dance floor, both of them twitching in movements inspired, apparently, by faulty electric wiring. He also spots Dawn, standing by a signed photograph of Gloria Gaynor, and concludes – a flashing moment, a thunderbolt revelation – that in the history of romance, no greater love has ever blossomed. Undaunted by the breakdown in communications that took place shortly after he punched Dawn in the eye, his eyes fix on her chest and he finds, perhaps for the first time, that he and his brother share an aesthetic judgement. Whatever Dawn has done to hurt him, he decides, can be forgiven, now and for all eternity.

'All right Dawn?'

Boom: first step, followed, Ricky knew, for sure, by a month of sweating, full-on shagging, followed by marriage and kids, big house in Barnet or somewhere, Ricky playing out at all the big mafia dos, ending up on Radio One and bollocks to old Mum, bastard Lee and his sad fuck father, RIP.

'Hello Rick,' says Dawn through clenched teeth. 'How's it going?'

'Tell you what, babe. This club is shit.' Ricky laughs until he hits the edge of hysteria. 'Fancy a drink?'

'You met my brothers?' says Dawn, tipping her head to one side to indicate a couple of megaliths bookending the cloakroom.

....

For a moment, Ricky feels a tremor of uncertainty. But whatever, all is love, drinks all round, my shout, future brothers-in-law no doubt, peace and goodwill to all men. Time to grab the moment.

'Let's all go,' he says. Bollocks to the DJ, who can fuck off back to Hatfield. Explaining the unstoppable demise of Ricky's Acciieeed Buzz!!! in swift précis form, he pays off Big Frank. A touch hard on his wallet, no question, but the omission would be seriously unwise.

'Are you all right, Ricky?' says paternal Big Frank. He casts a sideways glance at Dawn and her siblings. 'Watch your back, yeah?'

Emerging into glittering night, a tropic suburban nocturne, Ricky is cock of N15, a prince of the city. Cold blue neon light falls on sumptuous Dawn and her lithic brothers as they stand in a family threesome under the Cracker's sign, deliberating. A sign in itself, Ricky might have thought if chemicals had not been transmuting warning lights into fairy lights.

Instead, he grins the cheesy grin once more and asks, 'Where to?' Malleable to the point of idiocy, he feels himself becoming faintly cosmic as Dexter Wansell's 'Life On Mars' drops onto his personal, in-head jukebox.

'Nice pub down here,' says brother number one.

They turn into a dim side street off Tottenham High Road, Ricky overwhelmed by a silent soundtrack of shimmering Fender Rhodes, bass guitars thwacking like monstrous rubber bands, cymbals flickering in a sensory zone closer to light than sound. When the first blow comes, a real Nigel Benn into the kidney region, Ricky assumes it is a drum solo. Lenny White maybe.

'Cunt,' he hears. 'Cunt, cunt, cunt.' With each explosion of genital abuse comes a bass drum thud, a snare drum crack, a tom-tom roll. Aware that he is being kicked and beaten into a cheeseburger by the stone twins, Ricky can only feel joy. For years, he has tolerated the frustration of evading retribution, of skating the surface, of dodging the final judgement. What a pleasure to be caught and chastised for a life lived badly. Jaw sagging, rigid with the joy and pain that has overwhelmed him once again, he rolls over onto his back. Dawn is leaning over him and even in the moment of his greatest agony, he looks down the front of her dress and imagines the unimaginable. Lost in a world of incoherence, he riffles through the memory banks for the title of a track by Surface. 'Don't Have Sex With Your Ex.' That was it. Good track. Seven out of ten.

Oblivious to this impressive archival feat, Dawn reaches into her handbag – black rather than white he is pleased to note. All fingers and thumbs, she roots through tangles of that stuff women keep in their handbags, finally pulling out a small plastic bottle of the type that experienced tourists pack for holiday as detergent containers.

'Bastard, this is for messing up my face.'

She unscrews the top. Instincts still hovering between cosmic wonder and survival mode, Ricky closes his gaping mouth and screws his eyes shut. Liquid splashes his face. A cleaning product? Pine, not lemon. Pub toilets. The club shortly before opening time. Some brand of fucking bleach, anyway, which stings like fuck, whatever. He heaves himself up, pulls Mr Byrite's shirttail out of his jeans and rubs frantically at his face with a mixture of spit, blood and polyester. The family of his nemesis are vanishing back into the High Road, but since this phase of Ricky's great dream has also vanished, why bother? First priority is to avoid third-degree burns, or whatever damage a toilet cleaner can manage. Ricky seeks water and medical attention.

To his surprise, Cracker's accommodates him. Water, free telephone call, minicab to casualty, the dog's bollocks. A parting gift, as it were.

Six years later, Rick, as he now styles himself in his transformation, is stretched in a hammock roped between two stunted trees. Deep in the sandstorm beyond, shadowed figures, bare-chested and bare-breasted, mouths and noses masked by bandannas, twitch like deer on hind legs. Ferociously loud, bass drum and digital snare hammer their echoes of steel. An animated mural behind this pagan scene, the turquoise ocean sparkles with preternatural light. Rick's scarred face is burned to a deep red crisp. Hidden in a strip of undergrowth fringing the beach, he listens to the Arabian Sea and the drums, transfixed by their eternal thump and scrape and wash, and takes another long draw. Sitting in the dirt studying his boots is Philip of Zurich, techno backpacker, newly arrived from Europe via Paris and London. Undersea, over the sea, by the sea. Philip has yet to adjust to Indian energy, the heat, the parties, the new time zone. He reads and sleeps, sleeps and reads.

'What you reading?' asks Rick, who now hoovers up books and magazines, avidly if slowly, a Christopher Columbus sailing blind in the information ocean.

'Here,' says Philip, too jetlagged to concentrate, too tired almost to pass the book across to this fellow traveller and sudden acquaintance.

Perfect, thinks Rick. Short stories, music, clubs and drugs. He flicks and dips, picks out one with a title that rings rusty alarm bells, conjures memories of silhouettes under cold blue light. Sucking up the last grain of puff and sinking back in his hammock, he reads the

....

first line … 'The way it started out, Ricky was still cutting neat little two-inch slits in the bottom seam of his jeans …'

Something Changed

RICHARD SMITH

It's 1992 or 1993. Which seems like a hundred years ago now. Half eleven on a Sunday evening and I'm walking round to Michael's. I've just left my new boyfriend's flat. He thinks I'm going home. He's said he's going to leave me if I go round Michael's again.

Michael's eighteen. One of those boys that just brings out the mother in you. He was brought up in care and ran away to Brighton two years ago. He couldn't sign on so he sold his arse. Michael found out he was HIV positive when he was seventeen.

I met Michael at a club about a year before. Back in the days when everything still felt wonderful, just before our little dream fell through. He was always really caning it. The kind of boy who never knew when they'd had enough and never wanted the party to stop. Just like me. I loved Michael with that kind of love you don't waste on the boys you go out with. We were fierce friends. Sisters . . .

Friday night would usually end sometime on Tuesday back at Michael's old flat. When we'd spent all our money and duped every dealer we knew we ended up doing hot knives on his cooker till we both passed out. At least that's what we used to do. Now Michael's got into more serious drugs.

Rewind a couple of months or so. After our summer of love came our winter of malcontent. Winter always

....

turns a seaside town like this into a ghost town. Loads
of queens fuck off and whoever's left usually is pretty
fucked off. But that winter was the worst. A year ago
we were all still running around like love-struck teen-
agers. Everybody loved everybody else and all of that
guff. But now we were starting to get as rachety as
ex-lovers. Everybody started getting really vile with
everybody else. Ecstasy had brought us all together.
But now it was all falling apart. And a lot of people I
knew started falling apart too.

I can even pinpoint the exact night when it all went
wrong. It was this club's third birthday party. Just about
every fag in town had taken their first E here way back
in 1989 or 1990. But its glory days were over and
numbers had been trailing off for some time. Still we
all felt we owed a lot to this place and turned out to
celebrate its birthday the same as we would for any
other old friend. Everyone was looking forward to a
really big night out – 'just like the old days'. But the
dealer who supplied most of the dealers on the gay
scene had got busted earlier in the week so there was
an E drought on. A lot of people were on speed or
trips – which just made the uneasy atmosphere even
more strange.

I remember dancing near the end of the night and
just losing it completely. They turned the lights on but
the music was still playing which they never normally
did here. So, I figured with spectacular acid logic that
therefore I couldn't be in the club any more and must
be dancing someplace else. Maybe the middle of the
high street or outside the police station. At one point
earlier someone had passed me some poppers and the
rush from them made me trip that the whole club was
on fire. With hindsight that seems kind of fitting.

As ever we all went back to someone's afterwards.
Well that's not strictly true. That's what we used to do

....

back in the good old days. Now there were a lot of different gangs going off to a lot of different parties. You could tell how sour things had got that even at this one party different groups of people went off into different rooms. There was a lot of tension. It didn't help that just about the only drugs on sale now were these fucking vile microdots which loads of people were having bad times on. Me included.

I'm in the kitchen and I've finally gotten to talk to this beautiful French boy who's just moved over here. Fuck knows what he makes of us lot. Part of my trip is that I'm now convinced that I can't talk to anyone and I have to use my friend John as an interpreter. So I'm standing next to this boy and he's asking me pretty simple questions and I can't answer any one of them so just shrug my shoulders to say sorry. He's smiling politely and watching me stop every now and again to try and poke something sinister in my glass that no one else can see. Needless to say he goes home with someone else.

Eventually I snap out of the worst of it. Just as my friend John starts tripping out. He goes round telling everyone they're all invited back to his house. Great. He's got one of the DJs from the club to come and play and arranged to pick up this big bag of drugs from this friend of ours who deals. Suddenly John is everybody's best friend. But I know he's going through what I've just come out of. John tells me to go and pick up the drugs. I ask him if he is sure about this. Then he starts going round and asking people where they've hidden the bag of drugs. Oh dear . . .

I try and talk him down. Whispering to everyone as he's finished his little speech that 'there is no party, there is no bag of drugs, he's tripping off his cunt'. No one wants to believe this at first but they soon start leaving, their hopes that the night won't end just yet

. . . .

are broken. I really need someone to give me and John a lift in their car. We can't walk far with him like this and we really need to go someplace quiet until he comes down. Half an hour ago when everyone thought there was a party, getting transport was a doddle. Now people are just skulking off.

So much for solidarity. So much for our big friendships. So much for love.

Even the friendships that endured up until that bleak winter had started turning fucking weird. There was a gang of us round at Irish Brian's one night. We're all sitting round stoned when the doorbell rings at about four in the morning. Brian gets up and goes to answer it but doesn't come back. I can't tell if it's just the dope making me lose track of time. Then an ambulance pulls up outside. Brian comes back into the room. Says their friend Alan had sold a load of duff Es to him and his mates earlier. They complained and sort of shunned Alan at the club. He'd come round to apologise. Brian opens the door to see Alan standing there in tears. 'I'm sorry, I'm sorry,' he cries over and over. Then he holds up his hands. Alan had slashed his wrists. '*That's* how sorry I am . . .'

It was like the whole town was going through one massive collective comedown. So maybe it was inevitable that some queens settled on the classic comedown drug to see them through. Heroin.

Smack was always a secret. Queens will tell anyone who'll listen what a great night they've had if they've been tripping off their tits or speeding off their nut or were E'd off their face or stoned out of their box. But you never hear anyone boasting that they've done smack. As child-molesting is to sex, so heroin is to drugs. The last taboo. You keep it to yourself because

....

you know no one else will understand. And boys that start doing smack regularly soon stop going out.

It was strange how every queen that did it seemed to know all the others that did. And before long that was quite a lot of people. That winter we used to joke how you were more likely to see boys you knew down the DDU getting their needles changed than you were at any club in town.

The first time Michael and I tried it must have been around the end of that summer. It wasn't like we were really depressed or anything. We were just bored. And besides, we'd tried everything else.

The secrecy meant getting the stuff was a real bitch at first. Heroin users are reluctant to get others involved unless they're desperate for money. And heroin dealers are too wary to sell to people they don't know. We rang up one friend – he had the hots for one of us so we thought it would be okay – and asked him for the number of his dealer and told him to tell the guy we were coming and to tell him he knew us. The dealer wouldn't do it. Then we spent four hours traipsing round town trying to find this dealer's house that Michael vaguely remembered. Found it. Telltale smashed-in, boarded-up front window. Trade-mark big fuck-off dog barking its head off when we rang the doorbell. This young guy opens the door. 'We're friends of blah blah . . . (then *sotto voce*) can you sell us some smack?' He says he doesn't sell it. He's got some hash and pulls out this huge fucking brick. We buy some and bugger off. It's all been such a disaster we piss ourselves laughing all our way home.

Michael finally finds someone who'll sell us some late one Friday night. Neither of us has got enough money left. Michael's got a giro but he can't cash it now till the morning. We wait up all night watching shit telly

. . . .

and drinking worse whisky till the post office opens. Off we go . . .

You can't beat a nice ritual, can you? We pick the stuff up and pop into the 7–11 to buy a roll of tinfoil and a big bottle of Coke. Back to Michael's already glowing. So pleased with ourselves. Roll up a little tube out of the tinfoil and tear off some squares. Michael shakes a trail of smack onto mine. 'Ready?' I move the lighter up slowly underneath the line until the stuff melts and starts to run down the foil. I follow its trail with the tube and inhale the smoke. You never forget that bitter taste. Sit there and wait for it to start. Feeling a bit woozy. Feeling really nice. Feeling really slow. I walk over to the toilet 'cause Michael keeps reminding me I'm going to want to puke at any moment. Loads of real liquid stuff gushes out of my stomach. Four times. Best puke I ever had.

Then I'm sitting back down again, cuddling up to Michael. Slowly drifting off, occasionally nodding off, leaving his flat and going back to the womb. Me and Michael both look like we've just woken up. From time to time we'll turn our faces towards each other. 'Wuh?' Then smiling slowly put our heads back down once more. 'It's a bit trippy, isn't it?' I mumble as I listen to a bus shudder past Michael's window for what seems like hours. My mind floats off thinking about a thousand things, none of which matters. Fuck, this is so nice. It's just that at the moment everything's such a mess and everyone's being so shitty that feeling so calm's so wonderful. Perfect. No pain, no stress, no nothing. Just peace. And the peace goes on for ever.

Then the doorbell rings. We come to and Michael peeks out the window. It's a friend of ours called Murray. He sees Michael looking out so we have to let him in. I'm shocked by how easily I can snap out of it.

. . . .

We try to act straight but Murray clicks pretty quickly. He's not impressed. 'Oh, Michael . . .'

It was a good thing Murray came round really. Me and my new boyfriend are meant to be driving up North to visit my friend John and I've got an hour and a half to try and pull myself together. Oh yeah, I forgot. John left town not long after that party. So did a lot of boys I know.

I'm dreading leaving the house but I manage it okay. I feel sick. I feel like I'm walking the streets with a big sign pointing at me saying, 'Look everyone! This sad fuck's on heroin.' The boyfriend tells me how ill I look but doesn't cotton on. As we're getting in his car I have to stop. I crouch down by the bumper and start retching. I look up to apologise to the boyfriend and find there's now a policewoman standing over me. 'All right?' I tell her I'm really hung over. 'Too many beers last night?' I try not to laugh. She smiles – thank God – sees that the boyfriend's okay and goes.

It takes five hours and two stops while I puke to get to John's.

'Thanks for coming to visit me,' he says.

'Don't mention it.'

'Well no one else bothered,' he says, which kind of says it all.

Rewind back to Michael's on that Sunday night. Irish Brian and his boyfriend are here. One of the surprises about smack is how so many couples I know in fiercely close relationships are both doing it. They've lost their old flat – guess why – and are staying in Michael's other room. Michael's doing smack pretty regularly now. It's a bit like we're having an affair, me sneaking up here for a chat and a chase. Or, if I wasn't really stopping, just to burn what was left off the discarded bits of tinfoil on his floor. As the weeks passed Michael

. . . .

changed. And so did his flat. It's in a permanent state of darkness now 'cause he's pinned some patterned sheets over the windows. Slowly he's sold just about everything he had till all that was left was a mattress and a bucket for people to puke in stuck right in the middle of his living room.

Tonight's the night. Though I didn't know this before I got here. Michael asks me if I want to jack it up this time. We used to shoot speed sometimes before we went out – then stand in clubs being vile at a mile a minute while we waited for our telltale bruises to come up – but this was different. This was the big one. Course I do. I could never handle sticking the needle in myself so Irish Brian starts trying to inject me, but he's having trouble hitting a vein. Says it might be easiest to put it in my foot. I tell Michael to try. I really want Michael to do it to me. People always compare injecting to fucking 'cause they're both about having your body penetrated, but I can't see it. I just wanted to share my big moment with Michael, let him see how much I trusted him. How much I loved him. My life in his hands and all that kind of stuff. Drugs are all about the people you do them with. And maybe that's the problem with smack – it turns into such a solitary pursuit.

So in it went. Into my vein. And it was ... well, a bit of a disappointment really. I got bigger rushes when I was chasing it. But I'd done it now. In fact I'd done everything now. But I wasn't thinking 'This is it.' I was thinking 'That's it?' And 'That's it.' I'd done the lot.

The thing was, I could walk away. Which I did. There were always other things I had or wanted to do. But none of the boys I knew who stayed on smack for any time did. They were all long-term unemployed or on benefit 'cause they were HIV. They had a lot of time

....

on their hands. And heroin's a great way of killing time.

Michael started doing a bit of dealing to pay for his stuff. Started to get some strange people hanging round the flat. Like most queens I like a bit of rough, but there's rough and there's scary. 'There's no such thing as a straight smackhead,' Michael always used to whisper with a smile. I took his word for it.

I remember calling in on him one afternoon when I was passing. I knew something was wrong 'cause this time I caught Michael peeking out the window at me. He lets me in, but looks as embarrassed as we both had when Murray caught us. Michael is in a bad way. 'Oh Richard . . . will you come with us to the phone box?' I do. A two-minute walk takes ten. Michael's sweating and doubled up with cramp. He's in agony. He'd be screaming if he had the energy. What can I say? What the fuck do you say? I'm thinking to myself 'This is your fault, Richard.' But all I say is, 'Oh Michael . . .'

Michael didn't need me to tell him it'd all gone wrong. He got the council to move him and quit smack pretty soon after. Because most heroin users are young, straight men the drug's shrouded in macho myths – like how coming off the stuff's agony – going cold turkey and crawling up the walls crying out in pain for days on end. But coming off's pretty easy. Just as long as you want to. It's like Irish Brian's boyfriend Ben said to me after he'd kicked the stuff, 'Heroin's beautiful . . .', then a big pause as he stares into the middle distance at the memory, '*too* beautiful . . .'

I guess you want a happy ending. Well, we all calmed down a lot. Pretty much everyone I knew got clean. Eventually. Michael sat some O levels and got into college. But there's still a few boys I see when I'm walking round town who give me a smile and say 'hi'

. . . .

then rush right past before I get a chance to ask 'How are you?'

The funny thing is, we used to ask each other that question all the time when we were on E. But we were so off our tits we didn't really care what the answer was.

Biographies

MARINA BLAKE is an automechanic, glass-painter, singer, poet and fiction writer. She writes with equal fluency in both English and Spanish, and her poems have appeared in more magazines worldwide than she can list. Born in Illinois and raised in California and Mexico, she has also lived in England and Scotland. She currently lives in Phoenix, Arizona. She is interested in pornography, Tibetan Buddhism, splatter movies and Japanese poetry.

TONI DAVIDSON Born in Ayr, Scotland, Toni Davidson has previously edited *And Thus Will I Freely Sing*, Scotland's first collection of lesbian and gay writing. His short fiction has been published in *The Crazy Jig*, *Rebel Inc*, *A Queer Tribe*, *Gay Scotland* and *Queer Words*. He has recently completed a novel, *Scar Culture*.

BARRY GRAHAM Hailed by *Details* as 'one of the literary finds of the 90s', Barry Graham is a writer and performance artist and the author of several books. His novel *The Book of Man* was selected by the American Library Association as one of the best of 1995 and his essays and poems have appeared in newspapers and magazines on both sides of the Atlantic. He is a serious student of Zen Buddhism and ethnopoetics. He lives in Phoenix, Arizona.

BRENT HODGSON Born in New Zealand, 1945, and educated at Nelson's College for Boys, Brent Hodgson has lived in the UK since 1967. He came to Scotland for one week to see a friend and decided to stay a while, spending many a year recording those telephone numbers that are unique to public telephone boxes. His work has been published by *ASLS, B+W, Chapman*, Clocktower Press, *Dog, Epoch, Gairfish, Ireland's Own, Navis, Odyssey, Radical Scotland, Rebel Inc, Scots Glasnost, Scottish Child, Spectrum, West Coast Magazine, Witsnapper*.

STEWART HOME is the author of several books of fiction and cultural commentary including *Pure Mania, Defiant Pose, Red London, Slow Death, Cranked Up Really High: Genre Theory and Punk Rock*, and the editor of *Mind Invaders: A Reader in Psychic Warfare, Cultural Sabotage and Semiotic Terrorism*. In the eighties, Home worked as a visual artist before embarking on a three year art strike during which he read Hegel and watched kung fu videos. His writing and other cultural interventions are part of an ongoing project to reinvent world culture in its entirety. Home is single, lives in London and has never held down a steady job.

GARY INDIANA is the author of the hit play *Roy Cohn/Jack Smith*. His novels include *Horse Crazy, Gone Tomorrow, Rent Boy* and *Resentment*. He has also published two collections of short stories, *White Trash Boulevard* and *Scar Tissue*, and a collection of essays, *Let It Bleed: Essays 1985–1995* (Serpent's Tail, 1996). He lives in New York.

JOHN KING has had three novels published, *The Football Factory, Headhunters* and *England Away*. From 1990 to 1994 he edited the small-press magazine, *Two*

....

Sevens. Early influences include the Clash, the Sex Pistols and the Shed. In the latter half of the eighties he spent several years travelling abroad, with five months in India the highlight. He enjoys a drink, a curry and watching Chelsea play. He lives in London.

GORDON LEGGE was born in Falkirk and brought up in Grangemouth. He has published two novels, *The Shoe* and *I Love Me, Who Do You Love*, and also a collection of stories, *In Between Talking About the Football*. 'Moving Target' is taken from his forthcoming book of stories, *Near Neighbours.*

JEFF NOON Acknowledged as one of the most exciting new authors writing today, Jeff Noon has written four novels, *Vurt* (1993), which won the 1994 Arthur C. Clarke Award, *Pollen* (1995), *Automated Alice* (1996) and *Nymphomation* (1997). He also won the John W. Campbell Award for Best New Writer in 1995.

BRIDGET O'CONNOR has published two collections of stories, *Here Comes John* (Picador, 1993) and *Tell Her You Love Her* (Picador, 1997). She is currently the Writer in Residence at Newcastle and Durham Universities and is writing a novel.

RICHARD SMITH is a freelance writer. He won a special commendation in the 1994 ISDD (Institute for the Study of Drug Dependency) Median Award for his article on Ecstasy in gay clubs 'Us Boys Together Clinging' – which is included in his book *Seduced and Abandoned: Essays on Gay Men and Popular Music*. He also wrote the BBC Radio One documentary, *Lost in Music*, on how drugs have changed the sound of pop.

. . . .

LYNNE TILLMAN is the author of the novels *Haunted Houses, Motion Sickness, Cast in Doubt*, and *No Lease on Life*, as well as two collections of short fiction, *Absence Makes the Heart* and *The Madam Realism Complex*. She wrote the text for the *Velvet Years: Warhol and the Factory 1965–1967*, and was a co-editor of *Beyond Recognition: Representation, Power, Culture – Writings of Craig Owens*. Serpent's Tail recently brought out a collection of her essays, *The Broad Picture*.

DAVID TOOP is a musician and writer. He has published two books – *Rap Attack* and *Ocean of Sound* – and is currently writing a third: *Exotica*. He has also released three solo albums – *Screen Ceremonies, Pink Noir* and *Spirit World* (Virgin) – as well as curating a series of compilations for Virgin Records. He has recorded psychoactive shamanistic ceremonies in Amazonas, written interactive database material on shamanism and trance for the Shamen and worked with musicians including Brian Eno, John Zorn, Prince Far I, Jon Hassell, Derek Bailey, Talvin Singh and Witchman.

IRVINE WELSH Born in Edinburgh, Irvine Welsh is the author of *Trainspotting, The Acid House, Marabou Stork Nightmares* and *Ecstasy*.

ELIZABETH YOUNG is from Argyll, Scotland, and was educated there and in West Africa, London and York. She writes literary journalism for a variety of publications. She co-authored *Shopping in Space: American Blank Generation Fiction*, and has publishd a number of stories. She is currently compiling two new books. She lives in West London.

....